SIDETRIP TO SAND SPRINGS

SIDETRIP TO SAND SPRINGS

•

Kent Conwell

AVALON BOOKS
NEW YORK

PRINTED IN THE UNITED STATES OF AMERICA
ON ACID-FREE PAPER
BY HADDON CRAFTSMEN, BLOOMSBURG, PENNSYLVANIA

To every footloose drifter who has knocked about the world searching for a home, and to my youngest, Amy, who, in the summer of 2000, went out into the world. And, to my wife, Gayle, who always supports me.

Chapter One

When my old man died, he left me a deck of poker cards with the color worn off the back and a pair of down-at-the-heel boots. I suppose those two possessions were a fitting inheritance, for Pa was a drifting man with an obsession for poker. And that's what got me into a heap of trouble in Sand Springs, Texas.

The sun was straight overhead when my bay, Hardhead, and me splashed across a smooth flowing stream and rode into that tiny village about fifty miles west of Victoria. The day was hot and steamy. All I wanted was a thick steak, cold beer, and a hot poker game. At the time, that didn't sound like much.

What I got was a twelve-foot monster with one eye, three half-breed kids, a rundown ranch with three surly wranglers, and a spinster woman who had five thousand beeves for pets and liked to take potshots at men with her Kentucky Long Rifle.

Whenever I bellied up to the bar in a saloon, I always got the same question. "Where you from, Stranger?"

I always gave the same answer. "I'm from everywhere and going nowhere." That was usually enough for a laugh and free beer.

And it was good enough for the bartender of the Happy Jack Saloon in Sand Springs. He poured a cool one and slid it down the bar. "Drink up, Mister. Coldest beer west of Victoria."

At a nearby table, four citizens huddled deep in a serious conversation. They glanced up at me. I nodded and toasted the beer to them, "Gents."

They returned my nod and went back to their discussion. One of them kept fiddling with a deck of playing cards. From time to time, one of the others would glance curiously in my direction. I drained the mug.

After six hours on horseback on a steaming prairie under a scorching Texas sun, I was dry as a sunbleached buffalo skull.

Licking my lips, I banged the mug on the bar and bellowed. "That hit the spot, Barkeep. I'll have another." I slid the mug down the bar. He grabbed it in a meaty hand and waited, all the while grinning at me. I grinned back, fished a double eagle from my vest, and slammed it on the bar. "And buy one for those gents over there," I added, nodding to the four citizens. "Never let it be said Charley Bookbinder ain't a hospitable jasper even in a strange town."

That was the fast way to make friends in a Texas bar, and I had used the ploy more times than I could count. I wanted to be on friendly terms before I got anyone into a poker game. If I'd known then what I know now, I'd have chugged down that second beer as fast as I could and lit a shuck out of town.

I didn't, and like old Ben Franklin said, 'Experience keeps a dear school, but a fool learns in no other.'

That old saying fit me like fat on a hog.

One of the gents at the table spoke up. "Much obliged for the beer, partner."

"Mighty hot out," chimed in a second one.

"Yes, sir. Reckon it is," I replied, taking another long drink of beer.

To my surprise, within ten minutes, the five of us were joshing around like we'd known each other all our lives. This was certainly a friendly bunch of Texans, friendlier than most, especially so soon after the War of Secession when most strangers were suspect. I almost hated to take their money.

Then, to add to my sudden good fortune, I discovered I had not only stumbled on the richest man in town, John Lewis, who owned the local general store, but also George Markham, the mayor, Fred Turner, the sheriff, and Toby Reeves, town mortician and people doctor when he wasn't horse doctoring. If I'd ever drawn a full house, this was it.

I did some fast figuring. If I played my cards just right, I might ride out of Sand Springs with a nice little bundle in my pocket.

Sheriff Turner sipped his beer. "Where you from, Mister Bookbinder? Ain't seen you around hereabouts."

"Call me Charley, Sheriff. Charles Salmon Bookbinder. Mister Bookbinder was my Pa. His old soul has passed on. Me, I'm just Charley, and like I said, I'm from everywhere, and going nowhere." I sipped my beer, licked the foam from my lips, and added, "Truth is, I'm going to try to find me a little spread up north of Fort Worth. I been drifting long enough."

"You married, Charley?" Mayor Markham leaned forward.

I thought the question odd, but I dismissed it. "Not on your tintype, Mayor. Down near Brownsville, I courted a young lady once, but all her cups weren't in the cupboard, so I skedaddled right fast."

We all laughed at that. I leaned back against the bar and grinned. Yes, sir, this was sure a friendly bunch of Texans. They invited me to their table where one drink led to the next. We talked and shared lies.

Sheriff Turner excused himself. Ten minutes later, he returned. He winked at the mayor and nodded to Toby Reeves. I didn't think anything about it. I was too intent on getting those gents into a poker game.

Another round of beer showed up. We continued joking and laughing, and soon the ubiquitous subject of poker arose.

Toby Reeves paused in fiddling with the cards. He glanced around the table. "Well, fellers. Seeing as we're all enjoying ourselves, how about a hand or two of poker? See who pays for the next round."

A jumble of 'sures' and 'why nots' answered his question.

Toby dealt the first hand. I watched my fellow card-sharps carefully. Within one or two hands, I could usually tell just how good someone was.

Most of the time, I was the best at the table, though I tried not to show it. I was always careful not to win too much. A stranger cleaning out the locals didn't set any too well with most Texans. Fact is, that usually led to serious discussions about the proper thickness of various ropes for maximum flexibility or the right consistency of tar necessary to hold feathers.

I knew all the card tricks, but I never used them. On the average, most hombres at the poker table are better off back on the ranch wrangling steers or walking behind a plow.

But not my new friends. After only a few hands, I realized these old boys weren't fresh off the farm, so I knew I had to be patient. Three hours later, I was forty dollars ahead. That's when the roof fell in.

Mayor Markham dealt the next hand, giving me a pair of nines, a deuce, a four, and a queen. Betting started out slowly, but everyone must have had good cards for before you could click your tongue, the pot hit three hundred dollars. And we hadn't even discarded and drawn our cards.

I tried to still the mixture of concern and excitement. A pair of nines wasn't bad to draw to. Not top plank, but not bad. Another nine would give me three of a kind, a hard hand to beat. Considering the pot already had three hundred in it, and there was a good chance it would top six or seven hundred, I decided to stay.

Seven hundred was more than enough to get me on over to Fort Worth where I could pick up some big money and find that spread I'd been dreaming about.

On discard, I kept the nines. The mayor dealt me three new cards. If my mouth hadn't been closed, my heart would have jumped right out when I picked up my three new cards and saw another pair of nines. I tried to be nonchalant, but it's mighty hard to be casual when you're holding the dream of your life in your hands. I did my best.

The sheriff opened for ten dollars. I bumped it to twenty. Before I could catch my breath, Toby Reeves bumped another twenty. I stared glumly at my stash of twenty dollars on the table. Toby's raise had taken care of my last twenty bucks.

I suppose storeowner John Lewis figured he might as well make my misery complete, so he knocked the betting up another twenty.

The mayor showed no pity when he leaned back and stared at his cards. "Well, now, let's us take a look here," he drawled, studying his cards. "Sixty to me, huh? Well, boys, let's separate the wheat from the chaff. Here's forty more."

I looked around the table. What in the blazes was going on? They were betting like crazy men.

"It's up to you, Sheriff," said Toby.

I crossed my fingers that he would just call. Naturally, Sheriff Turner bumped it another twenty.

They all stared at me. "One-ten to me, huh?" I tossed in my twenty and held my hands out to my side. "I'm ninety light, boys. Would you be willing to take paper?"

The four frowned at each other, then John Lewis shrugged. Later, thinking back over it, I thought I'd spotted a faint grin on his face, but at the time, I didn't pay it any attention. "Sure. Why not, Charley? You seem like an honest gent of sorts." He fished a piece of paper and pencil from his pocket and shoved it across the table to me.

I studied my hand again. Four nines. I'd thrown away a queen, so there were only four or five hands that could beat me. I looked up at them. "Look, fellers, I wouldn't blame you if you said no, what with me being a stranger in town, but I owe ninety. I'd like to bump the pot, say fifty? What do you say?"

Toby Reeves arched his eyebrows. "Uh-oh, boys. Old Charley here must have the winning hand."

I grinned and scribbled out an I.O.U. for a hundred and forty dollars. I slapped it on the table.

The barkeep delivered another round of beer. I didn't remember ordering any, but I figured one of those friendly Texans had done it for me. I took a big swallow while the others continued betting like loco steers.

Then it was up to me. I realized I would be another hundred in the hole if I stayed in the game. I studied my hand, considering folding.

John Lewis put the spur to me. "You're in too deep to back out now, Charley. You probably have us beat."

I glanced from the corner of my eye at the others. The mayor was shaking his head; the sheriff chewed on his knuckles; Toby Reeves had a big grimace on his face; and John Lewis was clucking his tongue and rolling his eyes in misery.

Without hesitation, I wrote out another I.O.U. for a hundred. To my relief, no one raised me.

"Okay, Charley," said the sheriff. "What do you have?"

With a big grin I laid out the four nines. "Sorry, Gents. You win some, you lose some." I reached for the pot.

"Beats me." Store owner Lewis tossed in his cards.

"Hold it," chuckled Toby Reeves, spreading out four jacks. "Looks like I got it." He was the happiest mortician I had ever seen.

My jaw dropped.

"Not quite, Toby." Mayor Markham laughed. "Four kings whips up on four jacks anytime."

My jaw dropped lower.

"Both you boys hold on. We all looked around at Sheriff Turner. "I reckon I got me the winning hand," he said, laying down a royal flush, the ten, jack, queen, king, and ace of spades.

My jaw hit the floor.

The sheriff pushed back his Montana-crowned hat and dragged in the pot. "Thanks, boys. This'll put a few more beeves on my ranch." He looked around at me. "All right, Charley. It's settling-up time."

The table grew quiet. Four sets of eyes stared at me. All of a sudden, I had the distinct feeling something was wrong. I gave them a broad, good-old-boy grin. "Well, Sheriff. I don't have it on me. After all, you boys said you trusted me. Soon as I get to Fort Worth, I'll get the money back to you."

Still grinning like a possum, I looked at each of my poker pals, but they weren't grinning. My own grin faded.

Sheriff Turner shook his head, his hanging jowls flopping back and forth. "Well, now, Son. We do trust you, but not over to Fort Worth. You got anything here worth two hundred and forty dollars?"

I might not have been the sharpest needle on a cactus, but by now, I was getting worried. This game had taken a lopsided turn mighty fast. I held my hands out to my side. "All I got me, Sheriff, is my six-gun, an Army Colt; a Winchester 66, and my gear." I didn't mention the half eagle I carried in each boot for emergencies. Besides, they wouldn't even begin to pay off this debt.

He pursed his lips. "That your bay tied up outside?"

"Yep."

The sheriff studied the matter a moment, his face twisted in concentration. Finally, he grinned. "Tell you what, Son. That bay ain't worth forty bucks. Saddle maybe bring twenty. Same for the Winchester and that Army Colt, but I'll be generous and take them all and call us even." He looked around the table. "What do you boys think? Fair enough?"

They all chimed in just how fair they thought he was. I could have argued the matter. Here I was being left with only the clothes on my back. "But, Sheriff, that leaves me stone cold broke. No money, no nothing."

He grimaced and shook his head. "Blast. Reckon you're right, Mister Bookbinder. I didn't think about that."

I breathed a little easier, which by now I should have learned was a mistake. Around those four, a jasper never breathed easy. A smart jasper that is, which I obviously wasn't.

"Yes, sir, I plumb forgot, Mister Bookbinder. You see, all us honest and law-abiding citizens here in Sand Springs got laws against common loitering and panhandling. If you got no means of support or any ready cash, I reckon I got no choice but to toss you in jail."

Chapter Two

"In jail?" I stared at him in disbelief.

"Yep. For six months."

"Six months?" My head was spinning.

"Yep."

I looked around the saloon. Yellow patches of sunlight lay across the floor. The bartender was busy wiping down the bar. Two cowpokes sauntered in and ordered a beer.

"Jail," I mumbled. "Six months?" I looked at the other three. They stared back at me coldly. I turned to the sheriff. "Look, Sheriff. That penalty seems mighty harsh, but I was brought up to be law-abiding. I don't agree with this, but I reckon I don't have any choice. I'm willing to face my punishment, but six months in jail? Maybe someone here in town can float me a loan."

11

Toby Reeves shrugged. "Only one that could is the mortgage company, and when it comes to money, they're tighter than two coats of paint."

"Well, then, can't you point me to a job around here. I'm a good hand. I'll hang in there until I got you paid back."

The sheriff shrugged. "I don't see no problem with that, Charley. The Circle Bar needs a hand. Twenty a month and found. 'Course, old Jacob Walsh is a hard waddy to work for."

"Twenty?" I sputtered. "B-but, that'll take me to this time next year." I shook my head, unable to believe the tangled mess I was in.

Mortician Reeves spoke up. "Wait a minute, Sheriff. I might have a solution. The Bledsoe place." He looked at me. Hooking his thumbs in his black vest, he continued. "Probably won't take no more than a month or so."

I leaned forward eagerly. "What is it, Mister Reeves? I'll listen to anything."

He hesitated and then shrugged as if he were having second thoughts. "I don't know, Charley. Being a drifting man like you said, you might not be able to handle it. Or you might not even want to."

Sheriff Turner agreed. "Yeah, it'd be mighty tough, Charley. You might be best off taking that year long cowpoking job unless you'd just prefer cooling your heels in the clink for six months."

At the time I didn't notice how the sheriff casually kept tossing in 'six-months' and 'year long'. A couple of weeks later, I figured it out, but by then, he had accomplished what he had set out to do.

"Well, Charley," the mortician said. "You want to hear about it?"

I nodded emphatically. "You bet I want to hear about it."

He looked at John Lewis. "Maybe you should tell him, John."

The storeowner wiped his fingers back and forth across his lips, at the same time grimacing as if he had a mighty tough decision. Finally, he spoke up. "Well, you see, Charley, there is a little situation that needs some help. Not much, but a tad."

I glanced at the others around the table. From the innocent look on their faces, you could've sworn Gabriel had just planted wings on them.

"I'm listening."

"Well, north of town is the Bledsoe place. Old Ike Bledsoe settled it fifty years ago. Now, he was a good man. Peculiar in some ways, but good. Why, I could tell you a lot of stories about—"

Mayor Markham interrupted. "Tarnation, John. Stop rambling. Get on with the business at hand."

"Huh?" The storeowner looked around. "Oh, oh, yes, yes. Anyway, old Ike, he got stomped by a bucking bronc two years back and left the spread to his spinster daughter. She's a good person too, but she's what you might say sort of hard to get along with— sort of, ah, peculiar. Yeah, peculiar is a pretty good word."

I listened carefully, but I had no idea what point he was trying to make.

Mayor Markham gestured for John Lewis to continue. The store owner cleared his throat. "Now, on the Bledsoe Ranch is a fresh water spring, a mighty big one, one of them artesian springs that puts out a heap of water. That's what feeds that river right outside of town. You remember the one you crossed coming in?"

He paused, then decided to editorialize a bit. "That's where the town took its name. Of course, the water ain't sandy. In fact, it's kinda sweet tasting, but some of the townfolks thought the name 'Sweet Springs' too sissified and opted instead for 'Sand Springs'."

Exasperated, George Markham broke in. "John, you're going to keep us here all night. Just sit back and drink your beer." The mayor turned to me. "Here it is, Charley. Matilda, that's her name. Well, Matilda thinks she can run the ranch, but she can't. What few wranglers she has ain't worth shooting. Fact is, I'd be surprised if they ain't stealing her blind. Now, she's trying mighty hard, but the place is falling apart. She's missed the last few payments to the Great Northeast Land and Mortgage Company, which is run by Silas Henry and Ballister Fenton, two sneaking Yankee carpetbaggers trying to steal this whole valley from us. They already run the bank out of town, and now they're trying to close us down. We all depend on the spring water. If they take over her place, they'll either shut the spring down or charge us a premium price for the water. Either way, we'll have to shut down Sand Springs." He paused, glared at John Lewis in triumph, then added. "We want you to go out there, get a job, and straighten the place out."

All I could do was stare at them in disbelief. Finally, I found my voice. "But I ain't no cowman."

Mayor Markham explained. "We ain't got much time, Charley, and you're all we got."

"What do you mean, I'm all you got? What about the jaspers around here?" I pointed to the two cowpokes at the bar. "Why don't one of them go out there and straighten things out? Huh?"

"Why, that's easy to explain," Sheriff Turner said. "She shoots at them with her daddy's old Kentucky muzzlcloadcr."

"Yep," John Lewis put in. "And she's dead on at four hundred yards." He shook his head in admiration. "Old Matilda, she can outshoot just about any man hereabouts in Sand Springs."

Old Matilda! I sagged back in my chair. Suddenly, I saw a way out. "Well, boys, I hate to disappoint you, but if she drives townsfolk away, people she knows, what do you think she'll do when she sees me, a complete stranger?"

I had them then.

I thought.

Sheriff Turner cleared his throat. "We got that figured out, Charley. I'm going to take you out there and tell her the truth, that you lost your shirt in a poker game, and your fine is working for her the next month."

By now, I was grasping at straws. "But, what can I do in one month? That ain't long enough for much of nothing."

"Remember, we told you her daddy was the first to settle here?" Toby Reeves explained. "Well, he has more than ninety to a hundred sections of land up there."

"Yeah," the mayor put in. "Right next to the *Diablo Paisaje*. Bad things up there."

I wasn't much on the Tex-Mex lingo, but best I could figure out was that the expression meant *the devil's land* or *landscape*. Something like that.

Toby Reeves shot the mayor a hard look. "That's just old wives' tales." He looked back at me. "Pay him no attention. Anyway, old Ike's outbuildings and the main house are run down something bad, but he's probably got five thousand head of cattle running wild. Could be a sight more. No telling where all the stock is. Now, we got word that a cattle buyer is coming through here in exactly thirty-four days. He's paying ten dollars a head. Two thousand head will pay off her note at the mortgage company."

Mayor Markham finished the explanation. "So all you got to do, Charley, is gather two thousand head of her cattle in thirty-four days."

"With her say-so," I said, reminding them that it was no certain done deal.

"Naturally. Otherwise, we'd be forced to consider you a thief," replied the mayor.

I rolled my eyes. I was sinking deeper every minute.

"And if you're successful, Mister Bookbinder," Sheriff Turner added. "You'll be free to go, and on top of that, all this is yours." He laid his hand on the heaping mound of money in the middle of the table. "Over eleven hundred dollars."

"Eleven fifty to be exact," John Lewis added. "Of course, two hundred and forty of that is your paper, Charley. You can still leave here with over nine hundred clear."

"Oh, Sheriff, by the way," Toby Reeves said. "You better tell him about the kids."

"Kids?" I shook my head. "Come on now, Sheriff. I sure don't know squat about kids."

He waved my protests aside. "These ain't real kids, Charley. They're half-breeds. Old Ike, he was rough and quick-tempered, but he was a real softie for kids. He took these three in a few years back. They'd be ten, twelve, something like that. We ain't seen them in a couple years. You just need to know they're up thereabouts somewhere so you won't go shooting the first Injun you see."

"Yeah." Toby Reeves laughed. "Old Matilda. I don't think she'd cotton to you shooting one of her brothers."

"What . . . What if they don't have any particular use for white men?"

John Lewis laughed. "Oh, I don't reckon you'll

have any problem there, Charley. Just keep your eyes open and sleep with your handgun at night."

I squeezed my eyes shut and dropped my chin to my chest.

Sheriff Turner prompted me. "Well, Charley. What's it going to be?"

Without answering, I rose and staggered across the room to the bar. I glanced back at the sheriff. "Buy me one last drink?"

He nodded to the barkeep. "Whiskey. The best you got. Nothing is too good for our friend, Charley Bookbinder."

The bartender poured a single shot and started to pull away. I reached over and tilted the bottle until I had a tumbler filled to the brim. Taking a deep breath, I tossed it down.

Toby Reeves spoke up. "Look at it this way, Charley. You're actually coming out ahead. You don't have to go to jail or spend a year cowpoking. All you got to do is thirty easy days out at the Triple X. That's all. Thirty easy days."

John Lewis clucked. "You can do that easy, Charley."

"Yep," Mayor Markham chimed in. "Easy, easy, easy."

Somehow, the fact those old boys had all that confidence in me having it so easy didn't make me feel any better. But I was boxed in. Steep walls on each side and a herd of stampeding cattle behind. The only choice I had was straight ahead. To the Bledsoe place.

"Okay, Sheriff," I said, turning back to him. "Let's get it done."

He grinned. "First thing in the morning, Charley. Too late today. Let's just sit and play some more poker."

"No thanks, Sheriff. I've enjoyed enough of Sand Springs hospitality."

They all laughed and reached for the poker cards.

Chapter Three

Next morning, the sheriff and me followed the river north. The countryside between Sand Springs and the Bledsoe Ranch was rolling hills and broad valleys choked with lush bluestem and switchgrass. The country reminded me of the rolling hills north of Fort Worth where I sort of hankered to settle down.

As long as I could remember, my Pa and me never stayed in one place too long. I never knew my Ma. Pa said she was pretty as a honeysuckle bloom and had a voice like the meadowlark. He never told me much about her Ma and Pa, but I always had the feeling they weren't too pleased that Ma had married Pa.

Pa had been an orphan from eight on. I reckon that accounts for his restless feet and drifting nature. Somewhere along the way, he'd picked up on reading and writing, so he made sure I could do the same. He always had stories by a man from back east named Poe. They were spooky stories about hidden letters and gorillas and cats that made a body stop and try to cipher out the solution. Kind of teased the brain. I always liked them, although I never could come up with the right answer.

When I was thirteen, at least best I could figure, Pa and me made camp in the mesquite a couple miles south of Cuero. He went off to a poker game one night at a saloon and never came back. I wasn't too worried at first. He got himself drunk regular like. Sometimes, he was gone two or three days.

When he did that, I usually lazed about camp, gathering firewood when I needed it, shooting meat when I got hungry, even tracking animals just to pass the time.

Pa always came back. But that time, after a week, I began to worry. I decided to ride into Cuero the next morning.

That evening, I built up a fire, put coffee on to boil, and fetched my pony in closer to camp. While I was staking that slab-sided, spavined sorrel in some fresh graze, I heard a voice out in the mesquite. "Hello there fire."

I was smack-dab in the middle of that period in my life when my voice was changing. Pa had never laughed at me about it, but I was still self-conscious. I lowered the pitch of my voice as much as I could. "Come on in," I shouted back, cringing when my last word broke into a high soprano.

The sheriff rode in, a weather-dried whipcord of a man. The firelight flickered on a sun-darkened face that seemed frozen in a twisted grimace. He sat easy in the saddle, leaning forward, his arms stiff, both hands on the saddle horn. "You be the Bookbinder boy?"

I nodded.

Then he told me about my old man. "He was shot dead over a disputed poker hand. Some said he was cheating, but we found out that was a lie. It was some other hombre's doing all along. He got strung up that night."

I felt as if I was standing on a rise looking down on myself, all numb and dazed. I shook my head. "My Pa never cheated, Sheriff. He never had to."

His grim face smoothed out into a sad smile. "I know, boy. That's what I just said. The town found out the other hombre lied, and they strung him up. I was over to Goliad. I just got back. I wouldn't have known about you out here if the bartender hadn't mentioned that your Pa said he had a boy waiting south of town."

I can still remember the tears stinging my eyes, but I wasn't about to let anyone see me scrubbing at them. "Thanks for telling me, Sheriff."

In a gentle voice, he replied, "The townfolk took up a collection. They buried him in the town cemetery. I can take you there if you got a mind to."

By now, the sun was down and a cool breeze was blowing through the mesquite. Overhead, stars poked through the deepening gray of dusk. "Much obliged, Sheriff. If it's all the same to you, I'll ride in tomorrow morning."

"Stop by my office and pick up your Pa's belongings, you hear?"

"Yes, sir."

For the next fourteen years, I drifted. I lost count of the lonely nights I pulled up on a rise overlooking a cabin with yellow lights shining out the windows and tried to imagine what it must be like inside with a family. Christmases, Thanksgivings, Fourth of Julys, I usually spent in saloons.

One day, I ended up near a small town on the San Antonio River. From where I was camped in a clearing on a small rise, I watched as a man, his wife, and two youngsters, all dressed in Sunday best, bounced along the dirt road in a buckboard pulled by two frisky horses. On the way to church, I reckoned.

And that's when I decided I was tired of drifting. I'd once spotted a couple of nice sections north of Fort Worth. I told myself that if I ever settled down, that would be the place. I reckoned now was the time, so I headed northeast until I rode into Sand Springs.

At the crest of a hill, Sheriff Tucker pulled his pony up and nodded toward a cluster of buildings in the middle of a sprawling valley to the north. At that distance, I couldn't make out too much about the buildings, for giant oaks spread their limbs over the roofs. A wide stream meandered through the middle of the valley, the same one that ran along beside Sand

Springs. Clusters of beeves covered the valley like warts on a toad. "Well, Charley, there it is, the Bledsoe Ranch, the Triple X." He glanced over at me. "And good luck."

I studied him a moment. We were about the same height, but he had me by about seventy-five pounds. I could probably escape. My bay, Hardhead, was a hand or so taller than his gray. In the five years I'd owned Hardhead, I'd never lost a race.

That I could get away from Sheriff Turner I had no doubt. On the other hand, I didn't want to keep looking over my shoulder for the next few years. The truth of the matter was that I had done what Pa had warned me never to do, bet money I didn't have. And like Pa said, you want to dance, you pay the fiddler. The way I looked at it, I borrowed money, and now I was paying it back. "Thanks, Sheriff. I hope it all works out. You just be sure to talk to her before she starts shooting. I don't want . . . what's her name again?"

"Matilda. Miss Matilda. That's what she likes to be called. Miss Matilda."

I shrugged. "Okay. Miss Matilda it is. Just you be sure Miss Matilda understands I'm working off a debt by rounding up her cattle."

A sheepish grin played over his lips. He hemmed and hawed. "Well, Charley. You see, it ain't exactly like that."

Suddenly concerned, I frowned at him. "What do you mean, it ain't exactly like that? Either it is or it isn't. I'm not all that swift, Sheriff, but it seems to me there can't be too much of a misunderstanding about whether you want me to round up cattle or not."

"Well, yeah. Yeah, that's right." I breathed a little easier until he added. "Sort of."

"Sort of?" I started getting nervous. "I tell you, Sheriff. 'Sort of' makes me kinda antsy."

He took a deep breath. "Well, I reckon you deserve the whole truth since you're going to be in the middle of it like a hog in a mud hole. The truth is, Charley, Miss Matilda, she doesn't want to sell any of her cattle. She thinks the best thing for them is to let them keep multiplying and grazing, just grazing and multiplying. Like pets. You're going to have to find some way to convince her she needs to sell two thousand head."

All I could do was stare at Sheriff Turner in disbelief. Finally, I managed to put together a few shaky words. "Let me see if I understand this. I'm working for a lady who doesn't want me, who would gladly shoot me before she sat down to supper, and I'm supposed to round up two thousand head of her pets she doesn't want to sell and then take them to Sand Springs to be sold? Is that about it, Sheriff?"

He pursed his lips, ruminated over my question a few seconds, then gave me a casual nod. "Well, yeah, Charley. I'd say you have a pretty fair handle on the situation."

I stared at him. I'd been snookered in the past, but nothing like this. "And I suppose if I backed out, I'd end up in jail, huh?"

He grinned. "Like I said, Charley. I think you got a pretty good handle on the situation."

With a groan, I touched my spurs to Hardhead. "Well, let's us get on in there, Sheriff. Don't want to keep old Miss Matilda, the man-shooter, waiting."

The last mile or so, I started thinking back over the events leading up to where I was right now. I couldn't prove a thing, but somehow, the whole situation seemed just too convenient to have come about by just a poker game.

On the other hand, I'd rather spend a month wrangling cows than six months cooling my boot heels in the clink. One fact I knew for certain, no one would ever get me in a poker game again with the sheriff and his cohorts. No one. Why, they had twisted the situation around so much they had me coming out the winner.

Suddenly, the ground erupted in front of us. Hardhead reared, his front hooves pawing at the air. Beside me, Sheriff Turner cursed a blue streak, and then the boom of a Kentucky long rifle echoed across the prairie.

"Blast that Matilda," growled the sheriff, yanking off his hat and waving it over his head.

I wheeled Hardhead about. "Don't she know you, Sheriff?"

"Yeah. It's you she don't know." He continued waving his hat. I squinted toward the ranch and spotted a small figure in the front yard holding a rifle. She lowered the muzzle slightly. The sheriff grunted. "It's okay now. Let's go on in."

"How do you know it's okay?" I wasn't convinced.

"I just know. Come on, Charley. Stop whining."

The closer we drew to the ranch, the more apprehensive I became. I blinked once or twice, not quite believing my eyes. When Toby Reeves said the place was falling apart, he wasn't lying, probably the first time that day the town mortician could claim he told the truth.

Weather had ripped shingles from the roofs, leaving black holes where rain could pour in and heat could whoosh out. Many of the battens had rotted away, leaving gaps in the walls of the buildings. Only a handful of rail sections remained intact in the corral. Most sections had one or more rails missing.

Falling apart? Toby was being generous. Caving in was a better description.

While I was no top hand, I could see that the ranch had once been a solid working spread. And I reckoned that if someone wanted to put in a heap of hard work, the place would make someone a right fine homestead.

I couldn't tell much about Miss Matilda as she stood in front of the ranch house on the hardpan and watched us ride up. From the way the boys at the saloon had carried on, I figured she would be seven feet tall and broad as a grizzly.

She was just the opposite. Short, a little over five feet or so . . . I guess what the fancy folks would call petite. On the other hand, that Kentucky muzzleloader she pointed at us made her appear a heap taller. Like one of them Amazons I'd read about.

Her dark hair frizzed out in every direction under the battered slouch hat she wore pulled down over her forehead. Her blue gingham dress was soiled and torn. She had smudges of dirt on her cheeks. A pair of scuffed boot toes stuck out under the hem of her dress.

Sheriff Turner reined up and removed his hat. "Morning, Miss Matilda."

Knowing he had experience with this lady, I yanked off my hat and plastered a grin on my face.

She glared up at him. "What do you want, Sheriff? I'm busy."

"Yes, Ma'am." He gazed around the dilapidated ranch. "I can see you are, so I won't take much of your time."

She turned her hard glare on me. I grinned, but it was probably a pretty weak one.

The sheriff continued. "Got a favor, Miss Matilda. This here jasper is Charley Bookbinder. Old Charley lost money he didn't have in a poker game. I started to toss him in the clink, but I got to wondering if you might be able to use a strong back for a month or so. No more than thirty-four days. Truth is, if you was to take him on, the town wouldn't have to feed him three times a day for the next six months. We all would be mighty beholden to you, and you'd get the benefit of his strong back. Everybody would be coming out ahead on this."

"Yeah, everyone but me," I muttered under my breath.

She remained silent, studying me. I put on my little-boy-lost face and sagged in the saddle like a rag doll.

She looked me up and down like I was a bull she was considering buying. "How do I know he's got a strong back, Sheriff? He don't look like he has a muscle on that skinny frame of his."

He hurried to assure her. "Oh, yeah, Miss Matilda. Don't your worry about that. Charley's got a mighty strong back. Given the way he plays poker, he ain't got many brains, so he has to have a strong back."

I shot the sheriff a dirty look. I was sure beginning to wonder about the honesty of that poker game.

Miss Matilda lowered her long rifle. She dragged the back of her hand across her cheek, smudging the spot of dirt. "I got help, Sheriff. Turk's my foreman. Closecut and Oklahoma Fats are my wranglers." She kept her eyes on me.

The Sheriff chuckled. "Yes, Ma'am, I know you do, but this here help is free. You won't have to cook up no more grub either because Charley here ain't a big eater. And he knows he'd got to give you a hard day's work every blessed day or he'll end up back in the clink. Ain't that right, Charley?"

I stared at him. He'd stripped me of my brains and my appetite. "I don't know, Sheriff. You think it'll be all right if I take an occasional drink of water from the stream over yonder?"

He frowned. My sarcasm had flown farther above

his head than an eagle could fly. Resigned to my fate, I nodded. "Yes, Ma'am. The sheriff's sure right. I got a strong back, and I don't eat much."

She studied me a few more moments, then hooked a thumb toward one of the ramshackle buildings. "Yonder's the bunkhouse. Throw your warbag in there. Then meet me out at the barn. We're patching up the corral."

"Yes, Ma'am." I gave Sheriff Turner a brief nod and rode over to the bunkhouse. Inside, the cabin was in worse shape than outside. Half a dozen roughhewn bunks lined the walls. The puncheon floor had gaps between the planks, providing a ready avenue for cold air, centipedes, snakes, and spiders. I reminded myself to make certain I shook out my warbag before climbing in at night and my boots before putting them on in the morning.

Larger animals, raccoons, possums, even bobcats had their own doorway at the end of the room in the form of a foot-wide hole in the floor.

In the middle of the room sat a pot-bellied stove surrounded by broken chairs, rickety boxes, and bent buckets. I glanced out a back window and spotted a tiny building on a rock foundation at the edge of the stream. I guessed it was the springhouse.

I tossed my gear on an empty bunk and headed back to the corral. In the distance, I spotted Sheriff Turner disappearing over the rise at the end of the valley. I shook my head and remembered something my Pa once said about "rats deserting a sinking ship." I don't know why I thought of that particular remark. Maybe it was a portent of what was to come. I hoped not.

Chapter Four

In the corral, Miss Matilda struggled to secure an oak rail to a corral post. Without asking, I stepped in and held the rail so she could wire it tight. Even then, the rail slid down the post. I held out my hand for the cinching pliers. "Let me try, Miss Matilda."

Eyes narrowing, she hesitated, then handed me the pliers. Resting the rail on my shoulder to hold it in place, I inserted one handle of the pliers through the wire looped around the post and made several twists, drawing the wire tight. I stepped back and the rail remained in place. I grinned at her. "You want me to do the rest of them, Ma'am?"

She looked at me with a mixture of surprise and disbelief, which she quickly covered. "Yes. Do the rest."

"Yes, Ma'am." Up close, and without the Kentucky

muzzleloader, she didn't seem the least bit formidable. In fact, I got the feeling she was almost fragile.

She left me in the corral then, disappearing into the cookshack which was leaning against the bunkhouse, sort of propping each other up. Moments later, a young Indian girl emerged from the main house and followed Miss Matilda into the cookshack.

I discovered later she and the young girl did the cooking for the hands.

Two hours later, three tough-looking cowpokes rode in from the north. I figured they were Miss Matilda's wranglers, and I was right anxious to talk to them about the beeves.

They gave me a cold look as they rode past. Tying up at the rail in front of the cookshack, they glared at me, then stomped inside. I decided to wait a spell before bringing up the subject of cattle to them.

Moments later, Miss Matilda stepped out on the hardpan in front of the door and shouted. When I looked up, she waved me over. "Dinnertime," she shouted as I crossed the hardpan to the shack. She used the back of her hand to push aside the strands of brown hair plastered to her damp forehead. "Cornbread, beans, and beef. Got cold water or coffee, your choice."

She stood aside as I stepped into the dark shack. The three cowpokes had gathered at one end of the sawbuck table around the steaming pot of beans and platters of cornbread and beef, poking grub down their gullets like starving wolves.

One reminded me of a tree trunk. The muscles of his arm stretched the plaid shirt like dried rawhide. His blocky face was thick with a stiff black beard.

The light-haired hombre next to him was no bigger around than a rope. His sunken cheeks were dusted with a thin, sandy beard. Their cohort across the table carried a few extra layers of fat, enough to give him three chins. His nose looked like a red cucumber.

"Howdy, boys," I said pleasantly.

Two ignored me. The third, Cucumber Nose, shot me a hostile look.

The young girl stood in front of the stove, stirring a pot of boiling water. Miss Matilda indicated a stack of tin plates and a pile of flatware. "Grab a plate and help yourself," she instructed, pointing to the pots and platters of grub.

My belly was scrubbing up against my backbone, so I didn't hesitate. I poured some coffee and sat at the table. "Smells good," I said, just making conversation. "How about some of the beans and beef, Gents?"

They ignored me.

I've always been easygoing, but that didn't mean I let poor-mannered jaspers run over me. If they didn't want to slide the grub down the table, then I'd get it myself.

Standing, I reached in the middle of those surly wolves and grabbed the pot of beans. I ladled a couple heaps in my plate, plopped the pot down heavily, and reached for the plate of beef, deliberately reaching across Cucumber Nose's plate.

He jerked his head up and pushed my arm away. "Hey."

At his exclamation, his compadres looked up, angry frowns contorting their faces.

I figured they were trying to intimidate me, but I paid them no attention. "Sorry, Friend. Just trying to get some grub. I'll ask louder next time." He glared at me, but I kept an affable grin on my face while I forked beef in my plate. I handed him the plate of beef. "I'll take some of that cornbread over there, if you don't mind."

Surprised, he fumbled to take the plate of beef. "Huh? Oh, yeah. Yeah." He set the plate down and handed me the platter of cornbread. I took a couple while he held it. "Thanks, Partner."

Paying him no attention, I sat back down and proceeded to put myself around the meal, which to my surprise was right tasty. I glanced around the cabin.

The young girl was fishing plates from the steaming water and drying them off. Miss Matilda was rolling out some dough. I wondered if she was going to make a pie. "This is lip-smacking good, Ma'am," I said with a mouth full of grub.

She looked around in surprise, then a right becoming smile played over her lips. "Why, thank you, Mister Bookbinder. That's right nice of you to say so."

I nodded. "Yes, Ma'am." What was it the sheriff or one of my poker buddies had called her, a spinster?

Well, if she were a spinster, then I reckoned someone had gone and changed definitions on me. She was a right handsome woman.

I turned back to my grub. My three fellow cowpokes glared ominously at me. It was my turn to ignore them. Miss Matilda and the young girl left before we cleaned up our plates.

No sooner had they walked out the door than Tree Trunk growled. "What the blazes you doing here, Stranger?"

I took my time chewing up and swallowing the mouthful of grub I was working on. I looked around slowly, fixing my eyes on his coldly. "First, Mister, it ain't any of your business, but since I'm not looking for trouble, I'll be happy to tell you that I'm here because this is Sheriff Turner's way for me to work off a gambling debt."

The threatening expressions on their faces softened, then faded into smug grins. "Gambling debt?" The skinny one snorted.

I poked another chunk of beef in my mouth. "Yep. Wrote up some I.O.U.s I couldn't cover. Sheriff figured a month out here ought to pay for it."

Tree Trunk laughed. The other two joined in. "They call me Turk, Turk Warner. This here stringbean is Closecut. The one across the table is Oklahoma Fats."

"Mine's Charley," I replied without missing a bite of grub.

They kept watching me, and I kept ignoring them. Finally, Turk spoke up. "Well, Charley, since you ain't gonna be around but just a month, let me give you some friendly advice. Just mind your own business and don't do no snooping round."

I looked up from under my eyebrows. They were all staring at me. Suddenly, I had a bad feeling about rounding up those steers. Something in Turk's tone told me he might not be any too excited about me gathering a herd.

Dragging the back of my hand across my lips, I reached for my mug of coffee. I drained it, then grinned at them. "Boys, all I'm wanting to do is put in my thirty days doing whatever the boss wants me to. Then I'm out of here faster than a turpentined cat."

My answer seemed to satisfy them. They rose, dumped their plates and flatware in the pot of boiling water, and departed. I cleaned up my plate a few minutes later, dumped my dishes, and ambled outside where I rolled a Bull Durham cigarette and enjoyed it in the shade of a spreading oak.

The July afternoon was sweltering, but by supper, I had finished the corral. After putting myself around a heaping plate of grub, I strolled back out to look over my handiwork. I pulled out a bag of Bull Durham and rolled me a cigarette. I had some thinking to do. To the west, the sun had slipped beneath the horizon, painting the sky with purples and golds prettier than any picture I had ever seen.

Well, almost the prettiest. There was that one time on the Canadian River last spring when I spotted a young Comanche maiden on the banks of the clear flowing river. The sky was blue as a robin's egg, with a few puffy white clouds. Over her head, dark green cottonwood leaves riffled in the breeze. She wore an ankle-length buckskin dress bleached white and decorated with beads of every color imaginable.

If I'd been one of those artists who paint, that would have been the one picture I would have wanted to capture. To me, she was everything that was clean and pure and free.

The cawing of a crow snapped me back to the present. I stared at the sunset, thinking of just how contented I would be if, instead of me standing here with one boot propped up on the bottom rail of another jasper's corral, I were rocking on the porch of my own place, looking out over a few hundred head of fat beeves grazing on a broad prairie.

My mind wandered over the job I had ahead of me. I wasn't sure how Miss Matilda would feel about me gathering her pets to sell. Regardless of what the sheriff and his cronies thought, I didn't figure she would like the idea. So, I had to come up with some sound reason for selling them. To the average, logical hombre, keeping the ranch from being repossessed would be reason enough. I hoped it would be for her, but I had an unsettling feeling that sort of logic would not appeal to her.

After I built my second cigarette, Miss Matilda and the girl returned to the cookshack. A dim, yellow glow lit the cabin.

I smoked my cigarette and watched the two go about cleaning up the dishes and making the place ready for the next morning. I had just stubbed out my cigarette when the lights went out, and she and the girl headed back to the ranch house.

By now, dusk had deepened. Miss Matilda glanced in my direction and paused to speak to the girl. Moments later, the girl continued to the main house while Miss Matilda came toward me.

She had a little bounce in her walk. I couldn't help noticing she'd brushed her hair down some so that it was not all frizzed like before. She was probably a right pleasant woman when she wasn't toting that Kentucky muzzleloader around.

"Well, Charley," she said as she drew near. "You did a good job on that corral. Looks like it'll hold up for a spell."

"Thank you, Ma'am," I replied, surprisingly uncomfortable. I couldn't remember the last time anyone had paid me a compliment. "Just a patch job, Ma'am. That wire won't hold up all that long what with rust and all." She was close enough that I could make out the frown on her face and the way her little button nose kind of wrinkled when she frowned.

I explained. "Best bet is to drill holes and peg the rail to the post. Better still, get some rough sawn beams and fasten them between double posts set in the ground."

She chuckled wryly. "Sounds mighty fancy, Charley. Where do you reckon I could get all that money?"

"Well, Ma'am, I suppose you might consider selling a few head of your beeves. Sheriff says you got a heap to spare."

The smile faded from her face. She glared at me. "What the sheriff says don't mean nothing to me. Nothing at all." She spun on her heel and stomped across the hardpan to the main house.

I winced. Yep, I had a tough row to hoe ahead of me.

By now, the stars were out, sparkling white against a sky black as the bottom of a well. When I heard her door slam in the darkness, I headed for the bunkhouse. I had a full day tomorrow.

My bunk was typical of make-do bunkhouses, oaken poles fastened together with interwoven ropes drawn tight. I folded my canvas cover and laid it on the ropes. I spread my blankets on top of the canvas.

For a drifter like me who was used to the ground, that bunk was like a feather mattress.

During the early morning hours, a faint noise awakened me. I opened my eyes a slit. A silhouette stood between me and the open window. Oklahoma Fats. He was buckling on his gun belt. I didn't move. Moments later, a shadow hovered over me, and I smelled someone's rank breath.

I closed my eyes and continued breathing normally. Moments later, the creaking boards in the puncheon floor told me the three were leaving. I toyed with the idea of creeping out of bed and seeing just why they were skulking about in the middle of the night, but decided against it. As long as they didn't interfere with my job, I wouldn't interfere with theirs.

Chapter Five

After breakfast next morning, Turk and his compadres rode out. I remained behind, suggesting to Miss Matilda that maybe I should do a little patching on some of the buildings.

She hesitated, as if the idea of repairing anything was foreign to her. I pointed out the missing battens on the cookshack and bunkhouse as well as the holes in the roof. "Save firewood come winter, Miss Matilda. Like it is, I reckon heat runs out of those buildings faster than water through your fingers."

She frowned. "You think you can? I'd been wanting to get all this repaired, but the boys claimed they just didn't have time."

That struck me as curious, but I kept quiet. I wondered what could be keeping the three so busy that they had to leave in the middle of the night and kept them from making needed repairs about the ranch. "Yes, Ma'am. If you have the materials, I can do it."

Her smile grew wider. "Pa has a pile of materials in the first stall in the barn. He covered it with canvas. I think you'll find all you need." She glanced around at the young girl washing dishes. "Beth here can show you. Can't you, Beth?"

The small girl looked around. She had black hair and the finely chiseled features of her Indian blood. Her eyes were blue, a stark contrast to her dark complexion. She glanced at me, then dropped her gaze. "If you want me to."

Miss Matilda hugged the girl to her and explained, "Beth is my sister. Pa adopted her seven or eight years ago when she was just a toddler."

I rose and nodded. "Pleased to meet you, Beth. My name's Charley."

She looked up and gave me a self-conscious smile. "I know."

Matilda laughed. "Go show Charley the materials, Beth. I'll finish up in here."

In the barn, I uncovered stacks of battens and several piles of hand-split shingles.

By mid-afternoon, I had replaced all the battens. Then I started on the roof of the main house. To my surprise, Miss Matilda was right there handing split shingles up to me.

Work progressed rapidly. By noon of the second day, I had reached the last section of the barn roof, the shed under which our ponies fed at night. Wiping the perspiration from her forehead, Miss Matilda stepped back. "Turk told me they wouldn't be in for dinner, Charley. Beth and me will whip up some cornbread and get some cold milk from the spring house."

I grinned down at her. "Sounds mighty good, Ma'am."

She moved dinner out under the shade of a spreading oak. "We can get a nice breeze out here," she said, plopping down a platter of cornbread and a pitcher of cold milk.

I smacked my lips over the milk. "Long time since I had cold milk."

She and Beth smiled. She nodded to the springhouse. "We have a big artesian spring up in the hills. It's almost freezing when it comes out and it's still mighty cold when it gets here."

For the first time since I'd met the young girl, she spoke up. "The boys and me like to swim in the pond." Her blue eyes danced, and she smiled up at Miss Matilda.

"They try to get me to go with them," Matilda laughed. "But the water is too cold for me."

I swallowed a mouthful of cornbread soaked in milk. "Where are the boys? I haven't seen them around."

"Hunting," Matilda replied.

"They always have good hunts," Beth added.

"Deer?"

"Sometimes. Sometimes bear. Once they brought in two alligators," Matilda said. "They keep us in meat.

That way, we don't have to use more than one or two of our cows a year."

Pushing my empty mug back, I leaned up against the trunk of the oak and rolled a cigarette. "How old are the boys?"

Beth answered. "Jim is thirteen, Matilda says. Ben is almost. . . ." She hesitated and glanced at Miss Matilda who nodded encouragement. "Almost fifteen." She straightened her shoulders and added. "And we can read and write. Matilda taught us."

I arched an eyebrow, impressed. "Education is mighty important today, Beth," I said. "Mighty important." I looked at Matilda. "I reckon the boys are a big help to you around here."

Miss Matilda shrugged. "Sometimes. They're just boys. More interested in horses and hunting. I can't blame them. I'd rather be out racing horses and hunting than running this ranch."

I looked around. "This seems like a nice little spread."

She surveyed the ranch sadly. "Pa really kept it humming. Since he passed away, seems like something is always going wrong."

I leaned forward. "Oh. Like what?" I hoped I didn't sound too nosy.

"Diseased cows. Had to be shot. Other stock has strayed up into the *paisaje*. Turk figures that rustlers pushed them up that far."

Turk again. "You contact the sheriff?"

"He couldn't find anything, but he tried. There was

some sign, but the weather had washed most of it away. Sheriff Turner is a good man, an honest man."

Yeah, I told myself. Honest. But he sure didn't mind railroading a drifter like me into a no-win job. "He's always treated me fair," I said, feeling like a hypocrite. "How many head you figure you've lost like that?"

She stared up at the fluffy clouds overhead. "Oh, a couple hundred, Turk says."

I remained silent, but I had a feeling if I went looking for dead stock, I wouldn't find any. Chances were, Turk and his boys were driving the stock to buyers somewhere. Maybe Victoria. They couldn't be foolish enough to try to sell them in Sand Springs.

By the end of the day, I had finished the roofs. Now at least, we could keep the water and wind out.

Miss Matilda eyed my handiwork with satisfaction. "A good job, Charley."

"Thank you, Ma'am." I gazed at the buildings, but my mind was on the cattle. In the last couple days, I'd been looking for a way to bring up the subject of her beeves without seeming to be obvious. "Now that's taken care of, you want me to ride the property line? You can tell me how far your place goes. I spot any Triple X stock wandering, I can push it back in."

She considered my question a moment. "Turk and the boys are doing that, but I don't suppose another hand would hurt. Yes, why don't you do that, Charley."

*   *   *

That evening, I squatted outside the bunkhouse rolling a Bull Durham when Turk and Closecut stomped out. Turk glanced down at me. "You're a fair hand at patching up buildings, Mister. Reckon that counts for something."

Closecut snorted.

I touched a match to my cigarette. "Never hurts to be handy with your hands, my Pa always said."

Turk stretched his thick arms above his head. "Yep. Can't argue that." He pulled the makings from his pocket and rolled a cigarette. Oklahoma Fats sauntered out, and the three gathered in a small cluster by the corner of the cookshack, heads together. From time to time, one glanced at me, but I ignored them.

From the hard school of experience, I learned to pick my friends carefully. I'd already picked up some uncomfortable feelings about those three. Smart thing for me was to keep quiet and tell no one what I had in mind.

Next morning, I deliberately found some odd jobs in the barn until Turk and the boys rode out. They headed south. I went north, trying to remember the lay of the Triple X as Miss Matilda had laid it out for me the day before.

Five or six miles north of the main house, a valley ran east to west. The north side of the valley jammed up against rugged and almost impassable ridges and escarpments of rugged limestone, cut into twisting puzzles by small streams and covered with gnarled stands of postoak and blackjack, hackberry and hickory in which an army could hide. A forbidding wasteland, this was the *Diablo Paisaje* the boys back in the saloon had mentioned.

Miss Matilda had cautioned me. "Superstition calls it *El Paisaje de Diablo*, The Devil's Land. It is ten miles east to west and fifteen north to south. Beeves get back in there, we never find them."

Beth, her blue eyes wide with dread and trepidation, whispered, "Terrible monsters live back in the *Paisaje*. I hear stories from my people of creatures with one eye. Tall as the trees."

Matilda chuckled and hugged the girl to her. "Remember what I told you, Beth. There's no such thing as monsters. Certainly none tall as the trees."

The young girl looked up. I saw the skepticism in her eyes, the conflict between legends and tales from the superstitious past and the worldly wisdom of the present.

Miss Matilda had continued. "My place borders on Jacob Walsh's to the west. He's a good man. But his son is hot-tempered."

I rode the east property line. Beeves were everywhere, but I was more interested in sign of stock leaving the property. I studied the ground, searching for evidence that Turk had been rustling cattle from Miss Matilda. Once or twice, I spotted sign leading farther east. I followed, but found nothing. Had I jumped to conclusions about Turk and his compadres?

By mid-afternoon, I reached the northeast corner of the valley Miss Matilda had told me about. Beeves grazed lazily, hundreds of them. Too many, I figured. Two bulls watched me, their tails stiff.

Bordering the north side of the valley was *Diablo Paisaje*, a vast landscape of fallen boulders, twisted trees, and tangled vines. I stared at the chilling wall of limestone. For some reason, uncontrollable shivers ran up my spine. If monsters did exist, this was where they would live.

Pulling up under an elm, I ground-reined Hardhead and loosened the cinch. Gave him a chance to breathe while I ate a late dinner of cold cornbread and beef, washed down with spring water.

I sat in the shade, leaning against the trunk of the elm, smoking a cigarette and staring at the forbidding wall of *El Paisaje de Diablo*, unable to shake the sinister feeling crawling under my skin.

The silence surrounding me was so profound that I could hear crickets begin chirruping. I raised my hand and snapped my fingers. The crickets fell silent. Minutes later, one started singing and then they all joined in.

Tightening the cinch about Hardhead's chest and belly, I mounted and rode west along the jagged wall of rocks marking the boundary between the *Diablo Paisaje* and Triple X, studying the ground for sign. Off to my left, Triple X beeves dotted the range that was beginning to look over-grazed.

The hard ground revealed little. For the first two

miles or so, I spotted nothing other than coyote and raccoon sign along with the sighting of an occasional bobcat and several deer disappearing into the *Paisaje*.

Once I found the tracks from unshod ponies. I peered back into the dark and twisting cut into which the tracks led, wondering if Ben and Jim, Miss Matilda's brothers, had made them.

Late evening, as shadows began lengthening across the valley, I reined up. Half a dozen beeves had entered the *Diablo Paisaje*, single-file down a narrow trail that disappeared into a tunnel of thick vegetation. Glancing back south, all I could see was waving grass and grazing cattle.

I looked back up the narrow trail, chewing on whether I should follow the beeves into the dark tunnel of underbrush or not. This wasn't part of my job. All I was supposed to do was gather cattle, but I was curious. I didn't believe in ghosts or spooks, but the spectral impression exuded by the rugged landscape drew me forward. I dismounted and donned my leather chaps and buttoned my rawhide vest against the thorny vegetation. I swung back into the saddle. Taking a deep breath, I turned Hardhead into the trail. Immediately, I was swallowed up by gloomy shadows.

Briars and limbs scraped and snagged at me. The trail wound tortuously around house-sized boulders and through tunnels of low-hanging limbs.

Suddenly, I pulled up.

The trail of the cattle continued, but something had fallen in behind and was stalking them. I studied the new sign from my saddle. I'd never seen any track like it. More or less square in shape, it showed no toes. I wanted to study the track. I looked around before dismounting, shucking my Army Colt as I did.

I knelt by the track. Just a pad mark of some sort. I searched the trail, looking for more of the same, but the ground was too hard. Off to my right, a branch snapped. Moments later, another branch snapped directly ahead, this one much closer.

Hardhead snorted.

Swinging back into the saddle, I drew the reins tight and held the Army Colt steady on the trail ahead. My heart thudded against my chest. I peered into the underbrush. With a groan of relief, I spotted a deer through a window in the leaves of an ancient oak. The whitetail was about thirty yards distant. Abruptly, it froze, its head turned to my right, its eyes fixed on something I couldn't see.

Another branch snapped, and the deer bolted, spinning and leaping from my sight in less than a second.

A rancorous odor filtered through the underbrush, almost fetid, rotten. The movement to my right continued in the direction the deer had taken. Occasional branches snapped.

Hardhead quivered under me. Nervous, wary, he stutter-stepped backwards. I held him tight, my Colt cocked and ready. Through the window of leaves, I spotted underbrush moving as whatever was out there continued slowly on the trail of the deer. Gradually, the rank odor faded and drifted away.

I remained motionless long after the sounds and odors had died out. Then I realized I was soaking wet with sweat. I swallowed hard, and tugged back on the reins, backing Hardhead along the narrow trail to a spot where we could turn around.

While I wasn't a believer in ghosts or monsters, I knew something was in there, some kind of creature that I had never before seen. Not if it was the creature that made the tracks I had spotted.

Once out of the *Diablo Paisaje*, I breathed easier. At least out here, I could see whatever was coming at me.

By sunset, I had reached the western end of the valley, counting close to four thousand head of cattle. Three quarters of them carried the Triple X brand, the others, the Circle Bar, owned by Jacob Walsh.

The valley made up about a third of the ranch. If the numbers held, not counting the cattle from the next spread, Miss Matilda could be running close to seven or eight thousand head. Way too many.

Somehow, I had to find a way to convince her to get rid of two thousand head of her pets. Or more.

Chapter Six

That night, I camped some distance from the *Diablo Paisaje*, in the middle of three large boulders. I staked Hardhead out near the fire. I wasn't looking for ghosts, but at the same time, I wasn't forgetting that 'thing' back in there, the creature that left tracks unlike any I had ever seen. And in my twenty-seven years, I'd seen all the tracks from bear to elk, from wolverine to bob-cat.

I awakened regularly throughout the night, taking care to keep the fire burning brightly. I wasn't anxious for uninvited company.

Two times Hardhead whinnied, once just after midnight, the second, less than an hour later. I peered into the night in the direction he was staring, hoping to pick out eyes shining from the reflection of the fire, but with no luck.

After a few minutes on each occasion, Hardhead relaxed and returned to his grazing. I rolled up in my bedroll, keeping my Army Colt in hand and the Winchester at my side.

Next morning, I searched for sign, but found nothing. I studied the Devil's Land, the vast jumble of boulders, jagged upthrusts poking through tangled underbrush. In the distance, limestone hills rose against a blue sky. Not nearly as formidable during the day as at sunset.

One fact was certain, beeves roamed back through the maze of trails. I was curious as to how many, so after a short breakfast of coffee and leftover cornbread, I tied my gear behind the saddle and headed back into the threatening maw of *Diablo's Paisaje*.

I had only ridden a short piece before I stumbled over a beaten trail leading deeper into *Paisaje*. Pausing for a moment to pop the leather loop off the hammer of my Colt, I touched my heels to Hardhead's flank, and we stepped into another world, a world that within mere feet seemed to be pressing in on me.

There were no sounds other than the thud of my pony's hooves and the scraping of brush against my chaps. The trail twisted like a serpent, and at each bend, it forked. From hard-earned experience in caves, I took the left trail at each fork. The lay of the land always takes on a different look going than returning.

A mile or so in, I came across a box canyon half a mile deep and half that across, surrounded by limestone walls. The entrance was narrow, and I realized a couple of oak rails across the opening would create a natural corral.

I rode closer. Suddenly, I pulled up, my eyes fixed on the swath of cattle tracks leading from the canyon. Someone else had the same idea. I looked around. Lying in the underbrush beside the opening were four poles.

Looking around before I dismounted, I squatted by the poles. The bark was scuffed and worn on the ends. On either side of the entrance, I discovered fissures in the rocks where someone had inserted the poles as a gate. A worn trail led from the entrance farther north into the *Diablo Paisaje*.

I kept my eyes moving, studying the almost impenetrable underbrush surrounding me. I wasn't sure just what I had stumbled onto. At the same time, the situation could be perfectly legitimate, except I didn't believe that for even a minute. Why use a corral a mile deep in the *Paisaje*?

No. Until someone convinced me otherwise, rustlers had been keeping stock here until they could drive them out. And the first name that came to my mind was Turk Warner.

I swung back into the saddle and headed on down the trail, following the broad trail left by the cattle as the rustlers moved them north.

Best I could tell, the sign was several day's old. "Whoa," I muttered suddenly, pulling on the reins. In the middle of the trail just in front of me was the distinct track of a horseshoe.

I dismounted to study it, searching for some mark by which I could pick it out again, but I found no unusual marks on the shoe.

Farther on, the trail led past the escarpment I had spotted the evening before from the valley. I estimated the sheer walls to be at least two hundred feet high. Ancient oaks and cottonwoods grew along the base of the escarpment, and behind the thick cover, I spotted black openings.

Caves.

Sheltering what? Rustlers? I remembered the sounds from the night before, and the puzzling tracks. I continued following the sign past the escarpment.

After another hour, I turned back.

This time, I slowed Hardhead so I could study the few trails cutting from the main one to the escarpment. There was some cow sign as well as a few indistinct horse tracks. Nothing that appeared to have been made within the last week or so.

I examined the half dozen or so cave entrances from where I sat in the saddle. Only one allowed easy access for a man on horseback. The other entrances were three or more feet above ground level.

Shucking my Colt, I rode closer, noting faint sign leading to the mouth of the cave. I pulled up at the mouth and peered inside. Nothing.

Dismounting, I tied Hardhead to a willow and eased inside. My heart thudded against my chest despite no evidence indicating anyone was inside. A few feet in,

I found the remains of a fire. Weeks old, I guessed, stirring the ashes with my boot toe.

Around a bend, I spotted a lantern hanging on a peg in the wall. Lighting it, I was surprised to see a stack of firewood on the floor beneath the peg and four crude stalls complete with feed troughs and hay and oats strewn across the rocky floor. Whoever holed up here did it proper.

Keeping a tight rein on my suspicions, I muttered. "You can't tell, Charley. Maybe some of the cowpokes just hole up in here when the weather's bad."

I didn't believe that either.

I reined up when I exited *Diablo Paisaje* and looked back, surveying the wall of boulders and nearly impenetrable brush. No wonder superstitions and legends were born from it.

The *Paisaje*, while ominous enough in the dark, appeared nothing more in the daylight than what it was, a stark example of the devastating violence with which nature constructed the face of the earth.

What had me concerned now was if that violence extended beyond the boundaries of the vast wasteland.

I rode out, heading south. By mid-morning, as I ambled along the ridge that separated the Bledsoe spread from the Circle Bar, I spotted a large number of beeves grazing to the west in an adjoining valley. I studied the valley for riders. I wasn't too anxious to ride onto another man's property.

I took my time, rolling a cigarette and smoking it

to a nub before I moved. I saw no one, but I was curious about the beeves. Open ranges in Texas were mighty tempting to the wrong man. On some spreads, weeks passed between times that wranglers checked on their herds. More than one fortune had been made by jaspers swinging a wide loop and using a hot iron on mavericks.

Spooked as crib girls at a church social, the beeves scattered as I rode through them. They were mixed, both Circle Bar and Triple X. I guessed about three or four hundred belonged to Miss Matilda. I rolled another cigarette and headed back to the ridge, keeping Hardhead in a walk, noting how the bluestem seemed to be overgrazed in spots.

Back to the southwest, two riders appeared on the far side of the valley, riding hard in my direction. I pulled up on the ridge and waited, scooting around in the saddle and crooking my leg around the saddle horn. As they drew closer, I made out an older gent in the lead followed by one about twenty years the old man's junior.

They reined up several yards from me, their ponies lathered from the exertion. The older man's craggy face was square as a block. White hair stuck out from under his black hat, and thick pork chop sideburns grew down to his sagging jowls. The younger man was identical, except twenty years younger and seventy-five pounds lighter. Jacob Walsh and son, I guessed.

"Howdy." I nodded, careful to keep my hands in plain sight.

The younger man's hand drifted down to the handle of his six gun. "What the blazes you doing on our property, Drifter?" He reminded me of a barking puppy, but then, puppies have sharp teeth.

His Pa held up his hand. "Hold up, Boy. Mind that temper until you know what's going on." His blue eyes bore into me. "Who are you, Stranger? What are you doing out here?"

"Charley Bookbinder, Mister Walsh, if you are Mister Walsh. I work for Miss Matilda Bledsoe. She told me about you before she sent me to check on her stock."

His boy was spoiling for a fight. "Well, she should have had sense enough to tell where the property lines are. I don't like drifters coming onto our land."

I ignored him, but answered his question to his Pa. "She told me where the lines are, Mister Walsh. I been looking at all the stock around here. That herd yonder in your valley is about half and half." I hooked my thumb over my shoulder. "You probably have three or four hundred that drifted onto her place in that valley up north, the one next to the place they call *Diablo Paisaje.*"

Walsh studied me a moment. I spotted some reservation in his eyes. "You're working for Matilda, huh? Turk get you on?"

"Just met the jasper. Don't know nothing about him, and no offense, but I'd just as soon not. I'll be heading out of here in a few more weeks."

The old man drawled. "Well, reckon that speaks

sensible for you. You don't mind me being nosy, just what are you doing here if you're so anxious to light out?"

Sensing his dislike for Turk, I reached for my Bull Durham and began rolling a cigarette. "Don't mind a bit, Mister Walsh. You can thank Sheriff Turner." I offered him the bag. He seemed to relax. With a nod, he took it and began building one of his own. "Seems like I come up short in a poker game with the Sheriff and he decided I should wrangle for Miss Matilda for a month."

Walsh laughed and touched a match to his cigarette. "Sounds like Fred Turner." He gestured to his son. "This here is Jacob Junior. Got a little temper, but he's going to make a fine wrangler sooner or later."

I nodded. "Howdy."

Jacob Junior just glared at me.

The old man spoke up. "How come you didn't break Matilda's stock out and push it back over here?"

He seemed to be a fair enough hombre. I gave him a crooked grin and nodded to his son. "Being a stranger, Mister Walsh, I'm mighty careful. Some people shoot first and ask questions later. I got no hankering to be on the wrong end of those kind of questions."

He gave his son a disgusted look. "Sorry about him. Like I said, he's got a temper."

"That's his problem, Mister Walsh. Not yours."

Jacob Junior's face was red. He was ready to explode.

I continued to ignore the young man. "I got the feeling you don't cotton much to Turk or his boys."

He eyed me warily for a moment, then shrugged. "Ain't got nothing special against him. Seems like the three of them spend more time in town at the saloon than wrangling. The Triple X was a prime spread once." He tightened up on his reins. "Like I said, I got nothing against them. I wouldn't hire 'em. Just something about Turk." He reined around. "Tell Matilda I'll give her a hand separating out our stock whenever she wants to. In fact, I been thinking about selling some off. Some places are being over-grazed."

"I noticed. Appears to me both herds would do a heap better if they was reduced by about a third or so."

Pursing his lips, he studied the grazing beeves. "You know cattle, Mister Bookbinder. You're right. Our herds keep growing, soon we ain't going to have nothing for them to eat on. Tell Matilda to let me know when she's ready to separate the stock."

I crushed the butt of my cigarette on my chaps. "I'll tell her, Mister Walsh. Nice meeting you." I glanced at Junior. "Nice meeting you too."

Junior glared as I rode away.

Throughout the remainder of the day, I rode through once lush valleys, spotting herd after herd. I hadn't kept an exact count, but when a jasper runs across eight or ten herds each made up of three or four hundred beeves, he's seen quite a few. I'd guess at least three, maybe even four thousand, and that wasn't counting the herds back to the south of the main house.

Chapter Seven

I camped a few miles from the main house that night, not anxious to ride in after dark. Jacob Walsh had reinforced some of the first reservations I had about Turk and his boys. I had the feeling the Triple X foreman might be curious as to where I had disappeared.

I had run across nothing to suggest he and his boys were anything other than honest cowhands, yet his warning that first night about snooping nagged at me. If he wasn't up to something no good, why the warning?

And while Jacob Walsh didn't come right out and say it, the old man did have misgivings about Turk and his compadres.

Next morning, I woke with a start.

Two sun-darkened young men squatted by my fire,

staring at me. My first thought was to reach for my six-gun, but when I spotted the strips of meat broiling on spits stuck in the ground by the fire, I realized I was staring at Jim and Ben Bledsoe.

I grinned. "You fellers must be the Bledsoe boys, huh?"

The younger one, Jim, tended the broiling meat and eased the coffeepot farther into the coals. Ben rose, his face unsmiling. "You are the new one who works for Matilda."

"Yep. Name's Charley Bookbinder. You must be Jim and Ben."

The older one nodded.

I explained. "I been out the last couple days checking her stock back north."

Jim grinned at me. "We watch you."

Ben joined his brother in a big smile when he saw the surprise on my face. I shook my head and climbed from my bedroll, stretching my arms over my head. I reached for my gunbelt and buckled it on while I answered. "Well, boys. You got me there. I was always pretty slick about knowing who might be skulking around. Spent time with the Shawnee over in Central Texas. Figured myself to be about half Injun myself, but I reckon I was wrong."

I saw the smile disappear from Ben's face. He grew pensive. "Something bothering you, Ben?"

He glanced at his young brother. Jim grew somber. "Are you one of Turk's men?"

The question surprised me. I had the feeling I was

being given some sort of test. "No. The sheriff sent me out to work for your sister. I don't think Turk particularly cottons to the idea of me being out here. Personally, I don't care. All I want to do is keep your sister and the sheriff happy for the next three or four weeks."

Ben remained wary. "How can we know you are not lying to us?"

I studied him a moment. I could see the white man's skepticism in him. "Well, son, I don't reckon you can. You want to search me, you'll find I'm stone cold busted. Got nary a cent. Ride in and see the sheriff. He'll back up my story, or better still, ride in and ask your sister."

Jim chirped up, a grin popping on his face. "I believe him, Ben."

I saw relief in the smile that played across the older youth's lips.

I figured it was my turn now. "Why do you ask me about Turk? You don't like him?"

Ben shook his head. "No. He steals cattle. When we accuse him, he threatens us."

"Have you seen him rustling the cattle?"

Ben dropped his gaze to the ground. "No, but we have seen sign. It is plain, like the sun, there for anyone to see." Ben gestured to Jim. "This time Turk has said he will kill us if we come back."

For long seconds I pondered his remarks. "What about the sheriff? Have you told him your suspicions?"

Jim's smile vanished. "No one listens to half-breeds, Mister Bookbinder."

Ben broke in. "We can't tell Matilda. She would throw a fit, and Turk might hurt her and Beth. We decided it is best that our sister not know."

"So, that's why we're out here," added Jim. "We told Matilda we were going out hunting. Sometimes we've stayed away for two or three weeks on hunting trips before. We've only been gone a few days this time. She won't worry."

"Not for a few days," Ben added, the boys exchanging skeptical glances.

I gawked at them, unable to believe my ears. I heard myself asking, "When did he threaten you?"

"Last Monday. I saw him and the other two herding forty or so head of Triple X cows back to the southwest. They chased me. There is a valley of black rock, with many trails and caves. I hide in there." He grinned smugly at his young brother. "They could never find me in there, but I heard Turk shout out his warning."

"Warning?"

"Yes. That he would kill us. Afterward, I hurried back to the ranch for Jim. That's when we told Matilda we were going hunting."

"Yes. You came the next day with the sheriff," Jim added. "We thought you were like Turk and his men."

Ben straightened his shoulders. "It does us much good to know you are not like them. You will be at the ranch with our sister much. Do you think. . . ." He paused, searching for the words.

Jim spoke up. "She will need help. We cannot return."

I studied them several moments. Were they telling me the truth? Or was it simply an overreaction to the white man's prejudice against half-breeds?

Their eyes held mine. That convinced me.

A faint smile ticked up the side of my lips in a rueful grin. Now, not only did I have to gather two thousand head of cattle to save the ranch, I also had Turk's threat against the boys, maybe even Matilda or Beth. And probably me if I decided to lend a hand. I shook my head. All this because I wanted a poker game. But what choice did I have?

The boys had caught me in a short-deck poker game just like Sheriff Turner. "Don't worry, boys. No one will hurt your sisters."

They relaxed. Ben squatted by the fire while Jim handed us the broiled venison. After eating as much steak as I could put myself around and washing it down with a pot of coffee, I saddled Hardhead for the ride to the ranch. The boys stood, making no effort to ready their gear. "You're staying out here, huh?"

Ben shrugged. "What do you plan to do first?"

I swung into the saddle. "I'll keep my eyes open and see just what's going on. Turk and his boys go out at night sometimes. Probably won't hurt none if you followed." I hastened to warn them. "But don't let them spot you."

The boys grinned at each other. I had the distinct feeling they could track a grasshopper over granite without the grasshopper laying an eye on them.

I touched my spurs to my bay. He fell into a running two-step, a mile-eating gait. I had gone less than a quarter mile when I remembered the unseen creature two nights earlier, the rancorous odor, the snap of branches, the strange tracks. I grimaced, wishing I had questioned the boys about the creature, whatever it was.

I shrugged it off. I'd see them later. I could ask them then.

When I rode into the barn, Turk Warner's boys were waiting for me. As I dismounted, two figures leaped from the shadows and grabbed my arms. Before I could react, rough hands propelled me backward, slamming me against the side of the stall.

"What the. . . ."

Knocking around the country ever since I was a younker had provided me a heap of experience, both good and bad. I'd been in every kind of dogfight from brawls to shootouts. The one move I had learned was to act and act fast. Even if the move wasn't the right one, often a sudden rambunctious move surprised your opponent.

Instinctively, I dropped to my knees, then dug my toes into the soft ground and drove myself forward, yanking my two assailants off balance as I sprawled headfirst in the straw and manure.

With a shout of surprise, one jasper banged into the side of the stall and the other tumbled headlong in the straw. From under my eyebrows, I spotted a boot coming toward my face.

I rolled to the side and swung my open hand at the heel of the boot, knocking the hombre's legs from under him. He fell hard, flat on his back, striking with a thud and expelling a sudden gasp of air.

Still rolling, I shucked my six-gun, leaped to my feet, and quickly stepped over the sprawled body to the mouth of the stall.

The other cowpoke struggled to his feet, cursing.

"Hold it right there, boys," I growled, cocking the hammer. "I don't cotton to surprises, so my finger is about as tight as it can get against the trigger without something bad happening."

Oklahoma Fats glared at me. Still sprawled on the ground at his feet, Closecut shook his head.

I gestured to the dazed man with the muzzle of my handgun. "Help him up," I ordered Fats.

Grunting, the fat cowpoke struggled to hoist his addled compadre to his feet. Closecut leaned against Fats, trying to shake the cobwebs from his head.

"Now, what in the blazes is this all about? I'm not particularly partial to getting jumped like that."

Oklahoma Fats glared at me. A faint sneer curled his lips. "We thought you was a cowpoke from town we owed money to."

Closecut shook his head. He stared groggily at his compadre. Then he caught on to his partner's ploy.

"Oh, yeah, yeah. That's right. We thought you was him."

They were lying. "It ain't that dark in here, boys. Don't tell me you didn't recognize me."

Fats stammered. "Well, you see . . . we was . . . we was squatting in the shadows. I don't know about Closecut, but I couldn't get myself a good look at you, Charley. Why, if I'd known that was you, I'd never have jumped you."

I was at a dead end with them, at least, for the time being. Sooner or later, I'd learn the truth. With a nod, I holstered my Colt. "Well, mistakes happen. Sorry if I roughed you up some. You best get Closecut back to the bunkhouse. He looks like he's done been run over by a stampeding herd of longhorns."

After washing up in the river and slipping on a worn, but clean denim shirt, I paid Matilda a visit, bringing her up to date on the status of her herd as well as those beeves mixed in with Jacob Walsh's herd. She sat in a rocker on the porch in the shade. I sat with one leg hiked up on the porch railing. "Whenever you want to break them out, he said to let him know. He'll give us a hand. In fact, he's thinking about reducing his herd."

She looked up at me in surprise. "I can't believe Jacob would do that. Why, he loves his animals as much as I do."

"Yes, Ma'am. I know he does. That's why he's planning on thinning the herd."

A frown erased the surprise on her face. "But, why does he want to do that?"

I hoped I could explain it so she could see the benefit in doing the same thing. "Well, Ma'am, it's the graze. Up north, I figure you have three or four thousand head of beeves. I don't know about Mister Walsh, but I'd guess he has the same. They're eating the grass down to the root. When that happens, the grass don't come back. I know. I've seen it happen. The answer is to trim the herd. Say your spread can handle five thousand. More than that, they all suffer because all the graze is gone." I paused.

Matilda cleared her throat. "Well, I suppose I see what you mean. Of course, Pa was always selling stock, but I haven't. Are you sure about the graze?"

I dragged the brim of my battered hat through my clenched fingers. "You say your Pa culled the herd yearly. That's why the graze held up. But when you stop culling and the herd begins to grow, then the grass can't keep up with them. That's what has happened. Now, I know you certain don't want any of them to starve. But they will if we don't do some trimming like Mister Walsh. From what I saw up north, the graze will carry the beeves into the winter, but by the time your herd chews away on it this winter, you won't have anything for spring. What do you figure will happen to them then?"

She stared up at me. I could tell she wanted to respond, to refute my words, but she could not find an answer. Tears filled her eyes. Pressing her hand to her lips, she rose quickly and hurried into the house.

I should have felt good because now I was one step closer to building a herd for market, but for some reason I felt like a traitor.

Chapter Eight

After Miss Matilda ran inside, I hesitated, uncertain if I should wait or leave. In the past when a woman walked out on me, I usually knew what was coming next, but not this time.

Finally, I decided she wasn't coming back out so I ambled over to the cookshack. A thin trickle of smoke rose lazily from the tin chimney.

Beth had whipped up a pan of cornbread plus a small plate of fried venison. I poured me a mug of steaming coffee and heaped my plate with plenty of grub. Using my fork, I fished a small chunk of honeycomb from the honey jar and spread it over my victuals.

Beth stood at the pot-bellied stove, pleased to see the amount of grub I'd stacked on my plate.

"Smells mighty good," I said, sitting at the table. "Mighty good."

The slender girl nodded, her sharp blue eyes a right becoming contrast to her dark skin. "I hope you like it." Her words were soft and measured, as if she had been rehearsing them.

The cornbread was hot, but not quite as moist as that Miss Matilda had baked. Naturally, I kept my opinions to myself and just poured on more honey. "Just dandy, Beth. Just dandy."

After a few moments of silence, she spoke. "Did you see Jim or Ben?"

I nodded. "Yep. They're doing fine. No need for you to worry about them."

Her entire body seemed to sag with relief. She smiled brightly. "I am very glad to hear you say so. I . . ." Her face colored. "I am glad," she said lamely, turning quickly back to the stove.

I suppressed a grin. The undercurrents in her tone spoke louder than her words. "Don't worry. Those two boys can take good care of themselves."

"I know," she replied softly over her shoulder.

After dinner, I rode south, inspecting the graze. I knew what I would see, but I wanted to make sure. I had no doubt that the grass had been over-grazed at this end just as it had at the north end of the range. Within the first couple miles, I saw that I had the right notion. But along the way, I couldn't help noticing the decided difference in the number of beeves on the north range compared with those on the south. While I'd estimated around four thousand or so up north of the house, the numbers back south were nowhere near that size. Maybe two thousand or so.

The grazing beeves were fat and slick. They'd bring a top price at market. I remembered Ben and Jim's accusations against Turk. Maybe they were right. Maybe the muscle-bound foreman was rustling stock. That could explain just why the south range carried about half the number of stock as the north.

Back to the southeast, a line of dark clouds rolled over the horizon. I glanced at the dust rising in puffs from around the hooves of my pony. We could use some rain. A thin breeze cooled the sweat on my face. With the tip of my finger, I nudged my hat to the back of my head, exposing my damp forehead to the fresh breeze.

Ahead, a mile-long ridge of serrated limestone rose several feet above the meadow, a tumble of weather-smoothed boulders heaped along its shoulder. I reined Hardhead toward the end of the ridge when suddenly, something tugged at my leather vest. Moments later, the report of a rifle broke the silence.

Hardhead jerked around and reared. Another slug whined past my head followed by the booming of a rifle.

At the same time I threw myself from the saddle, grabbing the saddle gun as I tumbled to the ground, my brain was screaming 'Turk!' Startled, my pony bolted, and while the killer's attention was on my bay,

I snaked on my belly though the thinning grass to the protection of the boulders along the ridge.

Another shot tore up the ground several feet to my left. I clenched my teeth and narrowed my eyes. The shooter had no idea where I was.

Cursing Turk Warner under my breath, I squirmed on my belly to the crest of the ridge, about ten feet above the prairie. Peering between two small rocks, I scanned the ridge back to the west, searching for the slightest movement.

Suddenly, I spotted a patch of black in a small gap between two boulders. Slowly, I fit the butt of the rifle stock against my shoulder and lined up the sights on the black patch. Just before I squeezed off the shot, the patch moved.

I muttered a curse.

Abruptly, a head appeared and several rapid shots dusted off the boulders around me. One slug ricocheted off the limestone upthrust at my back and burned the seat of my trousers.

I jerked forward, then sent a string of curses along the ridge. "Okay, mister," I growled. "Let's see how you like it." I cocked the Winchester, took a deep breath, then lurched to the side and snapped off three quick shots.

Four more answered immediately, sending lead slugs ricocheting around behind me like a hive of bees. Chips stung one eye. I leaned up against the boulder and blinked several times. Tears filled my eye. I scrubbed at it.

Two more shots rang out, slamming into the limestone around me. I rolled onto my back and searched the countryside around me. My pony had stopped a hundred yards distant. He was grazing contentedly while I was getting my sorry hide shot up. Some loyalty.

I slipped down the backside of the ridge, and keeping my eyes on the crest, hurried along the tumble of boulders until I guessed I had moved behind the shooter. Taking care to move silently, I eased up the ridge, dropped to my belly, and peered over the crest.

I saw no one. The boulders lay strewn along the slope, baking in the afternoon sun. A tiny sparrow pecked the ground in the shade of one boulder. In the distance, a red-tailed hawk glided through the still air. I saw no sign of the shooter. Where in the blazes had he disappeared to?

The hair on the back of my neck prickled, sending danger signals racing through my body. I rolled over.

Twenty yards behind me, a lanky figure jerked a rifle to his shoulder. Frantically, I tilted the muzzle of my Winchester, hoping to throw a distracting slug at him.

In the next flicker of a second, he stiffened as the echo of a rifle shot broke the silence. His eyes grew wide in disbelief, and the rifle fluttered from his limp fingers. For a second, he staggered, then collapsed in a heap.

I jerked the Winchester to my shoulder and scanned the ridge. Thirty yards down along the crest, Turk

Warner rose from behind a boulder, his rifle smoking. He shouted. "Charley! You hear me? Hey, Charley!"

I remained motionless.

He called out again. "Hey, Charley. Are you hit?"

Lifting my chest from the ground, I held the Winchester over my head. I was still wary.

He nodded sharply and started toward me. "Did I get that jasper?"

I swallowed the lump in my throat and drew my tongue over my dry lips. "You got him. Who is he?"

Lowering his saddlegun, he shook his head as he clambered over the boulders. "Beats me. I saw him taking potshots at you. Looked like he had you dead to rights."

I relaxed, but I kept my Winchester cocked.

He stopped in front of me. "I heard about the dumb stunt my boys pulled while I was in town. Sorry." He grinned crookedly. "Looks like they were the ones who turned out sorry. That's why I came out here looking for you, to apologize for them. But they was telling the truth. Closecut owes a jasper in town forty-five dollars. The old boy threatened to whip up on him."

I had the feeling that Turk Warner had never apologized for a thing in his life, and if he was now apologizing, he had something in mind. "Like I told them, mistakes happen."

"Yeah." He pointed the muzzle of his Winchester at the dead hombre sprawled on the ground. "Like that one."

We stared down at my would-be assassin. His hatchet face wore a month-old beard. An old scar ran from his hairline down his forehead to the middle of his left eyebrow. A tomahawk or Indian warclub wound, I guessed.

"Thanks," I mumbled, still looking at Hatchet Face.

Turk grunted. "He's one of the bunch we been looking for."

"Huh?" I looked around, surprised.

"Yeah. This is some of the bunch we figure is doing some small time rustling." He pulled fresh cartridges from his gunbelt and reloaded the Winchester. "That's why I told you not to do any snooping around. Then you headed out north. I figured you might be one of the bunch rustling Bledsoe stock. We've been trying to catch them, but they've outslicked us good so far."

All I could do was stare gape-mouthed at him. His story was just the opposite of that told by Ben and Jim Bledsoe. And while Jacob Walsh had not accused Turk of anything, the old man had no respect for him.

"You mean, you're trying to run these rustlers down?"

He looked at me in surprise. "Why not? I work for the Triple X. They lose money, I lose money. That's why me and the boys sometimes go out at night in case you've noticed."

Embarrassed, I lied. "Oh? I never noticed."

Taking a deep breath, he looked around. "Your bay's back behind us. I'll fetch this old boy's sorrel, and we'll pack him into the sheriff. Let him decide what to do with the hombre."

I have to admit he had me confused. Usually, my first instincts about a jasper are right, but this time, maybe I had Turk pegged wrong.

I glanced back to the south. The rain clouds had broken apart. More dry weather. During the ride back to the ranch, Turk asked, "What were you looking for when you rode out north the other day?"

"Just taking a look at the lay of the land. Checking the grass and seeing if I could get an idea of how much stock Miss Matilda was running."

He gave me a sheepish grin. "Sorry about the other night. I come across rough to some folks. But the truth is, me and the boys are busting our britches to keep the Triple X going. We was afraid you was planning on cutting out a slice of the pie and hightailing it out of the country."

I couldn't resist a chuckle. "Nope. What I told you was the truth. Sheriff Turner put me to work here for a month. I can guarantee you that if he wasn't holding me here, I'd be over in Fort Worth by now."

"I know."

I looked at him in surprise.

He kept his eyes forward. "I was in town at the saloon this morning. That's all they was talking about."

Any cowpoke worth his salt is well aware that the center of communications in a small town is the saloon, then the Ladies Sewing Circle. Instantly, I became wary, wondering just how much talking was going on in the saloon.

"Oh?"

He kept his eyes forward. "Yep. Don't know if you figured it out or not, but you was in a fixed card game."

I looked around at him slowly. I'd wondered about that game. Things had worked out too convenient for the others and mighty inconvenient for me, but given the stature of the old boys I was dealing with, I couldn't bring myself to question it.

But now.

"Yep," he said, a sly grin cracking his bearded jaw. "They talked a heap, especially about two thousand head of cattle for the market."

I broke into a string of red-hot curses. "Who told you that?"

He glanced at me. His black eyes glittered. "Charley, some men are bigger gossips than most women. Two of your poker buddies was sitting around the table laughing about how they had suckered you."

I looked at him, puzzled. "Suckered?"

"Yeah." He turned to me, his thin lips curved in a tight smile. "Stacked deck." He shook his head. "The poker game that got you out to the Triple X. They needed a pigeon, and you was it."

I sagged back in the saddle, confused thoughts whirling through my head. I had wondered about the game. Now I knew.

He laughed. "Don't worry. Your secret is safe with

me. In fact, I've been trying to talk Miss Matilda into the same thing you are, selling off her stock. You been riding her range. You spotted the grass. Keeps up like this, next year they ain't going to be none and all her beeves will starve."

Despite my anger with Sheriff Turner and the others, I realized Turk had read my mind regarding the cattle.

He continued. "Tell you what. Four of us gathering stock can put a herd together easy enough. If you can talk Miss Matilda into it, we can get it done in a couple or so weeks. There's a natural corral up in the *Diablo Paisaje* that we can hold the gather."

I hesitated. Things were moving fast, too fast. I pushed the crooked card game aside and tried to focus on the present. Just this morning, Turk's boys were trying to stomp me into a mud spot, and four hours later, he had us working together as partners.

I didn't trust him even if he had saved my life. Jacob Walsh wasn't too keen on Turk, and the boys, Jim and Ben Bledsoe, claimed they spied Turk rustling stock.

I shook my head. I didn't know who to believe. I had a heap of thinking to do, and then I planned on telling Sheriff Turner just what I thought of him. As far as I was concerned, the town could dry up and blow away. I wouldn't lose a moment's sleep over it.

"Let me see what I can do with Miss Matilda," I said, putting him off. The truth was, at that moment, I didn't plan on telling her anything. I just figured on riding into Sand Springs and tie me a few knots in Sheriff Turner's tail and then ride out. "I think she'll see it's the only choice she has," I added so Turk wouldn't try to second-guess me.

Chapter Nine

Turk left me before we reached the ranch, cutting off for Sand Springs with the dead jasper. While I was unsaddling my pony, the supper bell rang. With a grunt, I slammed my saddle on the rack.

I had no appetite. Realizing that I had been suckered infuriated me. At least, the four of them could have given me a choice, but they treated me like meat on the hoof, pushing and cajoling me into whatever chute they wanted.

The stars came out, bright and sparkling. I stubbed out a cigarette and promptly rolled another. I made up my mind. Come morning, I figured on saddling up, riding into town, and telling Sheriff Turner just what he could do with my job. Let them find one of their own to put up with all the lunacies on the Triple X.

I resisted the tinge of regret nagging at me. I knew

Miss Matilda had problems, and chances were she would lose the ranch. But that was none of my business. I didn't owe her or the ranch even a Confederate dollar.

I was on my fourth cigarette when I heard gravel crunch behind me. I glanced over my shoulder. It was Miss Matilda.

"You didn't eat," she said, her voice tentative.

"Wasn't hungry." I shrugged, not wanting to look at her for fear she could read my face and see the decision I had made to ride out at first light.

She stopped at my side and laid a hand on the middle rail. "Beth cooked up a special pie, mock apple. It's quite a treat." Her wistful tone attempted to elicit my enthusiasm.

I glanced sideways at her. Even in the starlight, I could see she had prettied herself up in a fresh gingham dress with a white collar and cuffs. And her hair was fresh combed. I made an effort to be genial. No sense in stirring up her suspicions so she'd start asking questions. "I reckon it is. The boys probably gave it the dickens."

Miss Matilda laughed. "They did that. Do you want us to put you a plate aside for later?"

I turned back to the corral, staring at the distant stars perched on the horizon. "No. Thanks anyway. I just got no appetite tonight."

For several moments, we remained silent, staring at the darkening sky. She smelled fresh and clean. I caught a whiff of some kind of perfume. I had no idea what it was, but the aroma filled my nostrils.

"You've worked very hard the last few days, Charley. I truthfully didn't think it would work out when you and the sheriff arrived. I was wrong, and I want to you know, I appreciate all you've done."

"Yes, Ma'am." I kept my eyes straight ahead, wishing she'd stop being so nice. I still planned on riding out the next morning.

She tried to be casual. "You rode south today. What were the pastures like down there?"

I quickly gave her a terse rundown of the conditions plus an estimate of the number of beeves I had spotted.

"I see. Turk headed down that way today. He hasn't come back yet. I hope he isn't in any sort of trouble. Did you happen to run across him?"

"Yes, Ma'am." Keeping my eyes averted, I briefly told her about the bushwhacker and the fact Turk was taking the body into Sand Springs.

She gasped. "Are you all right?"

Before I could catch myself, I chuckled. "Not a scratch. I don't know who the dead hombre is, but Turk thinks he's one of the bunch that has been rustling from your herd."

"I'm glad," she whispered. Then hurriedly, she added. "I mean that you're okay. Not about the rustling."

I nodded again, keeping my eyes on the horizon. "Yes, Ma'am. I'm fine."

She was silent for so long, I finally looked around

at her. After a few more moments, she spoke. "How much stock do I have left down there?"

"Hard to say, Miss Matilda. Probably two, maybe three thousand. I reckon you'll have between five and seven thousand all totaled."

Even in the starlight, I could see the tears glistening in her eyes. I frowned, trying to imagine just what could have upset her. Finally, she wiped her eyes and cleared her throat. "And you say the grass down south is about the same as that up north?"

For some reason, I once again felt like a traitor even though I was telling her the truth. "Afraid so, Miss Matilda." I turned to face her. "I don't like upsetting you, Ma'am, but unless you make a move before winter, you're going to lose at least half your herd by next spring. Maybe more."

We grew silent. I stared off into the night. I heard her beside me, a soft sob, the silky rustle of cloth against skin as she wiped at the tears. Several minutes passed.

Finally, she cleared her throat. "Well, Charley. Much as I hate to say it, maybe we should talk about selling off some of the herd."

All I could do was stare at her.

I shook my head in disbelief at the peculiar tricks life played on an hombre. Here I was, ready to ride into Sand Springs the next morning and quit when all of a sudden, I had the two thousand head of cattle handed to me by their owner.

I couldn't decide whether to curse or laugh.

* * *

Sleep was a long time coming that night. I was upset over the high-handed treatment the sheriff and his cronies gave me. Yet, if I just held my temper a few days until the cattle were gathered, then I could ride away, richer by over nine hundred dollars. "That's a heap of greenbacks to throw away just because of pride," I muttered to myself, turning over in my bunk and pulling the blanket up around my neck. I dropped off to sleep, still undecided about what the morning would bring.

My eyes popped open early in the morning, at that time when sleep is soundest and the night is darkest. I lay on my side without moving, listening to the sounds around me, letting my gaze roam while I tried to figure out just what had awakened me.

Then I heard it again, muffled voices outside my window, too soft for me to discern the words, but not the urgency in the tone. I made out two, then three voices. Still motionless, I squinted into the dark at the other bunks. Oklahoma Fats lay snoring in his bunk. Who could Turk and Closecut be talking to? Why wasn't Fats part of the conversation?

After a few minutes, the conversation died away and Turk and Closecut crept back into the bunkhouse. Silhouetted against the window, Turk cast a glance in my direction.

* * *

Ten minutes later, both hombres were snoring loud enough to wake snakes. I rolled onto my back and stared into the dark above my head. The day's events ran though my head. I could still smell the dust whipped up by the rifle slugs and the smell of my own sweat.

Why had Turk saved my life? Because we wrangled together on the same spread? I didn't buy his loyalty pitch. The only loyalty Turk had was to money. So why had he stepped in? Not for me, but for himself. Why? The cattle?

The realization hit me like a prairie thunderstorm. So that was what he had up his sleeve. The cattle. He learned that my job was to gather two thousand head. He'd offer his help. If anyone spotted him, Turk could simply explain that I was doing a job for the sheriff, and he was giving me a hand.

Then once the cattle were gathered, he and his boys could run them off.

Hold on. Another thought hit. Run them off? To where?

Two thousand head was a heap more difficult to hide than half a dozen, which they could push over to Victoria in a couple days. Why take such a risk?

Of course. The cattle buyer. Turk was after the cattle buyer, not the cattle. The buyer was coming in with at least twenty thousand dollars. Maybe more.

Outside, a rooster crowed. I turned my head and stared at the dull gray of false dawn. Sitting up, I shook my denims and boots for spiders and centipedes before dressing. After breakfast, I'd ride into town, but now, I had no intention of quitting. I had over nine hundred dollars coming. Besides, I liked the idea of giving Miss Matilda a hand. She and Beth were good people. They deserved better than wranglers like Turk and his bunch.

Chapter Ten

The ride into Sand Springs was uneventful, although once or twice I thought I spotted a cloud of dust behind me. I pulled into a thicket of laurel beside the road and waited, but no one appeared. "Just my imagination," I muttered, reining my bay around and heading on into town.

Sheriff Turner leaned back in his chair and propped his heels on his desk, the rowels on his spurs gouging chunks from the battered top. Even stretched out, his belly hung over his belt, and his heavy jowls gave him the appearance of having no neck.

At his back were three empty cells, the ceiling of which was a loft for storage. The sheriff chuckled. "Well, Charley, I'm tickled to hear about the roundup, but you sure about Turk and his boys? Now, they ain't got too good a reputation among the church-going, but they ain't never caused no trouble here in town neither. Fact is, I ain't talked to Turk or his boys in months. That's how much they been behaving themselves."

I took a step closer to the desk and looked down on him. "Well, now, Sheriff. Being new hereabouts and all, I'm taking folks at their word. Both Ben and Jim Bledsoe say they saw Turk and his boys pushing forty beeves to the southwest."

The sheriff snorted. "Jim and Ben? Shoot, Charley, they're nothing but little half-breeds. Always trying to cause trouble. Wouldn't trust them to spit right."

I saw right fast I was getting nowhere with the sheriff, so I tried a different approach. "Then explain this to me, Sheriff. Why does Turk want to use that corral a mile deep in the *Diablo Paisaje*? I've seen it. There's a worn trail leading from the canyon farther north. And the caves along the escarpment have been lived in."

Lazily, Sheriff Turner pulled a sack of Bull Durham from his pocket and worked his fingers in the mouth of the bag to open it. "Beats me, Charley. Now, I ain't saying rustlers don't use the canyon. And maybe it is Turk and his compadres, but no one has ever come in here and accused them of rustling. And I ain't never found any proof of it."

A sense of frustration washed over me. I poured out the rest of my fears in desperation. "I don't think they're after the cattle this time, Sheriff. That cattle buyer is coming in with at least twenty thousand dollars. Maybe more. Sand Springs has got no bank, so he's forced to bring the cash. I'd almost be willing to bet you six more months at the Triple X that the money is what they're waiting for."

A grin curled his lips. He poured tobacco in the thin paper, spilling a few strands on his leather vest. "You're a real glutton for punishment, ain't you, Charley?"

From the corner of my eye, I caught a glimpse of movement. I looked around at the head-high barred window on the far wall. Nothing. Just clouds in a blue sky. Just my imagination, I told myself. Or maybe a bird.

"Well. What about it, Charley? You think you can take six months at that ranch?"

"Forget the six months, Sheriff. I just want to know if you can you set up some way to keep an eye on the cattle buyer?"

After twisting the ends of the cigarette and sticking it between his lips, the sheriff reached for a match.

It slipped from his fingers and fell through a crack in the puncheon floor. He muttered a curse. "Need to repair this blasted floor. Some of the boards you can yank up by hand."

He retrieved another match and lit his cigarette. Squinting through the smoke curling around his eyes, he added. "Tell you what though, Charley. I'll keep an eye on him, and on them. Okay? I think you're wrong, but I'll see what I can see. If they're up to no good, I'll find out."

I relaxed. That was all I could ask. "Thanks, Sheriff. I reckon we'll start gathering tomorrow."

"You got about three weeks before the buyer comes in. From here he's going on west, out to San Antone and north to Austin. Reckon those Easterners are getting mighty hungry for Texas beef."

I considered the information the sheriff gave me. If the buyer was going on to San Antonio and then Austin, he was probably carrying considerably more than twenty thousand unless he wired the rest of his funds to a bank in San Antonio.

One fact was certain as mud on a hog, that cattle buyer was going to be carrying more money than any jasper around here had ever seen.

Cutting through Jacob Walsh's spread, I swung wide of the Triple X, deciding to come in from the north through *Diablo Paisaje*. I was curious about the mysterious land, about the creatures in its midst. At the same time I hoped to run across Ben and Jim Bledsoe. We had some visiting to do. I trusted Sheriff Turner, but I figured he promised to keep an eye on Turk Warner just to shut me up until I gathered the two thousand head.

Ahead of me, several meadowlarks glided and dipped across the prairie.

Diablo Paisaje was a geological throwback to the prehistoric days my Pa once told me about. The churning of shifting plates had torn the earth apart, ripped deep crevasses in the rocky soil, hurled huge boulders for miles, and forced rocky escarpments into the clouds. Ferocious creatures of every shape and form roamed the devastated landscape.

Over the centuries, Mother Nature had struggled to cover the formidable landscape with tall trees, wiry grass, and thorny shrubs, a weak effort to soften the harshness of the primeval land.

As I approached the *Paisaje*, a feeling of uneasiness came over me. My bay, Hardhead, perked his ears forward as if in anticipation.

A wall of green and brown rose from the prairie, a city of forests and boulders that seemed to forbid entrance.

Along the north border of the *Paisaje*, as along the south, numerous trails led in and out of the rugged countryside. Keeping my eyes moving, I flipped the rawhide loop from the hammer of my handgun and reined Hardhead into one of the more heavily traveled trails.

Almost instantly, a gloom settled over me, and while I could see the sun overhead, it seemed to have lost much of its intensity.

I couldn't help noticing the lack of animals, of birds, of chirping. It was as if I'd entered a dead world. The only sounds were the dull clip-clop of my bay's hooves against the rocky hardpan.

The trail twisted around house-sized boulders, down

steep crevasses, and through thickets of head-high cactus with inch-long spines.

My neck began to ache. I massaged it, telling myself to relax. I was wound tighter than a corkscrew anticipating what lay ahead. Forcing a weak laugh, I mumbled to Hardhead, "Nothing here we won't see outside, boy. Just keep moving."

From the sign on the trail at my feet, riders were fairly common. The Bledsoe boys? Rustlers?

I felt rather than heard another presence.

Moving silently, I reined Hardhead into a copse of wild coralberries and stunted ironwood along a curve in the trail and waited. Moments later, I heard unhurried hoofbeats, then the murmur of voices. I shucked my six-gun and waited.

Soon, two riders passed, strangers. They rode slowly, dillydallying. Both wore beards. Drifters, I guessed. At least, they had the look of drifters.

I remained motionless, watching as the two disappeared around another bend. Finally, their voices died away, but I continued to wait.

Something nagged at me, an uneasy feeling, a puzzling awareness. I laid my hand on Hardhead's neck, gently patting him.

My caution paid off.

Around the bend rode the Bledsoe boys, Jim and Ben. They rode easily, casually, eyes on the trail. When they came up beside me on the trail, I snapped a twig.

Both boys stiffened slightly, but kept the presence of mind to keep riding.

Then I whistled and rode out on the trail behind them.

Ben glanced around and grinned. He reined up and nodded. "It is good to see you, Mister Bookbinder."

"Howdy, boys." I nodded to the trail down which the drifters had disappeared. "Look like you had some company."

The younger one, Jim, grunted. "Just following after them two. Seeing where they was heading."

Ben nodded to the underbrush from which I had emerged. " 'Pears to me that you learned your lessons good with the Shawnee."

"Thanks." I looked back to Jim. "Where'd you boys pick up them two jaspers?"

"The caves," replied Ben.

"Yeah. We smelled smoke last night. Those two had a fire big enough to roast a yearling."

Ben agreed. "I don't figure they were on the run with a fire that size. We smelled the smoke two miles away."

Before I had a chance to reply, Jim held up his hand. His black eyes locked on his brother's. "Listen."

I strained, but heard nothing.

Whatever it was, the two brothers heard it. As one, their eyes flicked over their back trail. Ben leaned forward and whispered. "Follow me." He walked his pony, a paint stallion.

Just around the first bend, he led us onto an almost

invisible path cutting away from the main trail. I glanced over my shoulder in time to see Jim slide off his dun pony and brush away our tracks.

Keeping his pony in a walk, Ben led us deeper and deeper into the *Paisaje*. Ahead, the escarpment reared its limestone bluffs high above our heads.

Far behind us, angry voices erupted.

Jim grinned at his brother. "Looks like they finally found where we left the trail. You'd think after all this time, they'd learn how to track."

With a chuckle, Ben touched his heels to his pony. "They'll never find us."

I leaned forward over the neck of my pony and whispered. "Who's they?"

Ben winked at his brother. "Turk and his boys. They keep trying to run us down, but we grew up playing in the *Paisaje* after Pa took us in."

I heard the sound of several horses crashing through underbrush far to the rear.

Ben chuckled. "Let's go. We'll have some fun watching them run in circles."

Remaining on horseback, Ben led us into the mouth of a cave behind a thick tangle of greenbriers and wild grapes growing from the base of the escarpment to the top. He retrieved a torch from a shoulder-high ledge and lit it. A flickering glow illuminated the cave, revealing a trail at the rear of the cave curving gently upward, higher and higher into the escarpment.

The trail finally opened onto a large room, one that had seen much use over the centuries. Black beds of charcoal marked where fires had once blazed. Dried straw and buckets of oats indicated where ponies had been tied. Across the room were several openings covered with a thick growth of vines. I knew exactly what we would see when we looked out.

Dismounting, we peered through the vines.

A hundred feet below, several horses trampled through the thorny underbrush. Curses split the air punctuated by screams of pain when a rider impaled himself on a thorn.

I recognized Closecut and Oklahoma Fats, but Turk was missing. The other three were strangers.

"They are the ones who drive the cattle to Victoria," Ben explained when I asked of them.

"We thought the two we followed earlier were part of their gang."

"But they weren't," Ben put in. "Just drifting through."

"What do you mean, they drive the cattle to Victoria?"

Ben gestured to the east. "We have seen those men take the cattle from the canyon and drive them to Victoria where they sell them at the stockyards."

My heart thudded against my chest. Maybe here was the hard proof I needed against Turk. "Who do they get the cattle from, Turk?"

Ben shrugged weakly. "We do not know. All we see. . . ." He held up four fingers. "We see this many times, those men take Triple X steers from the canyon and drive them to Victoria."

"But, they're with Turk's boys now."

Jim nodded. "This is the first time we've seen them all together."

Looking back down on the searching men, I tried to make out the features of the three strangers. "Where do they stay? Those other three, I mean. Here in one of the caves?"

Ben's eyes narrowed as he peered through the vines at the riders futilely searching the tangled undergrowth. "No. They have a cabin north of Victoria on the Guadalupe. About once every two weeks, they go to the box canyon back south. That's where they hold the beeves."

"I've seen it. It looked like it had seen a lot of use." My pulse raced in anticipation. "Have you ever seen Turk herd the stock into the canyon?"

Jim looked up at his brother sheepishly. "No," Ben replied.

"You sure? Never?"

"No. Just sign."

"What about his boys?"

Disappointed, the boys shook their heads.

"What about the forty head you saw Turk pushing to the southwest?"

Ben nodded. "We saw them."

"Where did they take the beeves?"

Ben's face sagged. "I do not know. We did not see them take the cows off the ranch. But we did find the sign where they did."

"But, you didn't see them?"

"No."

"You didn't follow?"

Ben ducked his head. "They see us. We left. A rain that night wiped away the rest of the sign."

I muttered a curse under my breath. We were getting nowhere.

I glanced around the cavernous room in which we stood as a thought struck me. "Is there a way out of here? Suppose they discover the cave."

A big grin replaced the dejection on Jim's face. His white teeth were a sharp contrast to the shadows of the room and his dark complexion. "They'll never find the cave. They've been at the opening, but they were too blind to see it."

"Beside," Ben added. "There is a way out at the back of this room." He nodded to the shadows in the rear. "Another tunnel leads out. This whole escarpment is like a spider web of caves."

Jim laughed softly. "Me and Ben are the only ones who know about them. Not counting you now."

I shook my head in wonder. "Well, boys, that's good to know. We might need them, because if what you tell me about Turk rustling stock is true, we could very well be looking for a spot to hide out, and a place to hide Miss Matilda and Beth."

Chapter Eleven

Jim was right. The searchers rode past the entrance to the cave three or four times without spotting it. Oklahoma Fats even stopped beside the web of vines and wiped the sweat from his porky face.

Finally, they gave up in disgust and took the trail back south, disappearing into the tangled thicket.

Ben looked up at me, his youthful face stern in its seriousness. "What brought you up here, Mister Book-binder?"

I reached for my canteen. "Call me Charley. And I came up here for the same reason you did. Turk."

The boys frowned at each other, clearly puzzled.

I related the events of the preceding day, of Turk's offer to help gather the stock, of Miss Matilda's decision to sell off the cattle, of my conversation with the sheriff, and finally, of my own suspicions.

Ben shrugged after I told him of Sheriff Turner's refusal to believe the boys' accusations against Turk. "The sheriff only believes the white man."

"That's one reason I'm here, boys. I've got to be sure where we stand."

"I don't understand." Ben shook his head.

The only way I knew to say what I had to say was blurt it out. "When we first met, you said he was rustling cattle, but you hadn't seen him, not with your own eyes."

Anger and resentment flared in the young man's dark eyes. "Like we said, the sign was clear. Even an old man with bad eyes could read the story."

More than once, I'd found myself neck deep in the hog wallow by taking folks at their word. I couldn't be sure if the boys' accusations were fact or the result of their hatred for Turk. Before I took any drastic measures, I had to be certain.

"And I'm sure you're right, Ben. The fact they're all riding together now is proof enough for me, but stop and think. As far as the rustling itself, all you have to go by is sign. We can't say an hombre is guilty of rustling just by association. Now, how do you think that kind of evidence looks to the sheriff or any other white man?"

The young man stiffened. "I do not lie."

I laid my hand on his shoulder. "I know, and I believe you, but can't you see? We need eyewitness proof that Turk is rustling. Let's get that proof, and they will believe you."

Jim snorted. "Even if we have proof, the white man will not believe us. We're half breeds. No better than animals."

I glared at the boy. "You're as good as anyone. Half breed or not, don't forget it. I'm white. You tell me you've seen them pushing Triple X cattle across the spread, and I'll believe you. Don't worry about the sheriff," I added. "He'll believe me. That's why I'm here. That's why I need your help."

Jim studied me a moment, weighing his answer. "What can we do?"

I looked at Ben. He nodded. I cleared my throat. "First, I want you to keep your eyes on the herd as we build it. You can stay out of sight. I don't think Turk will try anything, but I can't be sure. Turk doesn't trust me, and I'd bet a double eagle he knows I don't trust him. But him and his boys will help put the herd together. I'll take the help where I can get it."

"We will watch with the eyes of an eagle."

"Maybe he thinks to take the whole herd," Ben said.

I pulled out the makings for a cigarette. "Two thousand head is a mite harder to keep hidden than a dozen. I don't believe he's foolish enough to push a stolen herd that size fifty miles to Victoria. I think he's after the greenbacks the cattle buyer is bringing. That's what I told the sheriff."

The younger boy rolled his eyes. "The sheriff will pay no attention."

I grinned. "Then we'll pay enough attention for

everyone. You fellers just keep your eyes open. Look out for those hombres from Victoria. And you might pop into the barn every couple nights just so we can keep each other posted of what's taking place."

"Who will watch Turk, Closecut, and the fat one?"

I touched a match to my cigarette. "Let me worry about them."

Later, I cursed myself for not remembering to question the boys about the creature in the *Diablo Paisaje*. I was certain they knew of it even if they had never seen the animal. I could still smell the rancorous odor of the creature. I shivered.

Deliberately, I kept Miss Matilda in the dark about my suspicions concerning Turk. I didn't expect any problems during the roundup. Those would come with the cattle buyer.

The next two weeks passed quickly. Miss Matilda and Beth always had a rib-sticking breakfast piping hot for us, usually consisting of steak, gravy, and hot biscuits. What we couldn't put ourselves around each morning, we wrapped in oilcloth for our dinner on the trail.

Two or three times during the roundup, Sheriff Turner dropped in, sometimes to put himself around a plate of grub, other times just for a cup of sixshooter coffee.

The boys and I met regularly in the barn.

The roundup went as smooth as good whiskey. To my relief, there were no incidents, no problems, and most important, no sign of the three owlhoots from Victoria. Even Jim and Ben were surprised.

"I still think Turk plans to steal the cattle," whispered Ben that last night in the barn.

"Then why hasn't he tried something?" Jim frowned up at his brother. "I think you're wrong, Ben. It's like Charley said, Turk is after the money."

Ben snorted. "How can he get the money? Everyone in town knows the buyer's coming. He has his own riders, and the sheriff is watching." He shook his head. "Naw, I think he'll try to get the cattle somehow."

Verbally, I stepped between the boys. "We'll all rest easier when the mortgage company is paid off," I said. "Until then, we just keep doing what we've been doing. Watching Turk and his boys. If they try something, we'll be waiting."

Early next morning, we pushed the cattle out to Sand Springs, reaching the small town just before sunset. From time to time, I spied shadows drifting along the horizon. Ben and Jim were following us. I grinned. They were good men despite their youth.

In the west, the sun balanced on the black line of the horizon, ready to roll off and pull the night after it.

Accompanied by the sheriff, cattle buyer George Wiggins rode out to meet us, followed by eight or ten wranglers. Wearing a brown suit with stripes and a bowler hat that was better suited for the east than out here in Texas, Wiggins pulled up in front of Turk and me. He stuck out his hand and introduced himself with a broad grin. "My boys here will take the beef off your hands."

I nodded. "Sounds good to me."

He looked around for Miss Matilda. "I left the money in the safe over in the sheriff's office."

Sheriff Turner grinned and indicated two men in suits standing in front of the saloon glaring at us. The carpetbaggers who owned the mortgage company, one was tall and skinny, the other short and fat. "Yep. I got the money there, and it's about to drive old Silas and Ballister to drink."

We all laughed as the two continued staring at us.

"Is Miss Bledsoe around?" George Wiggins looked past me.

I hooked my thumb over my shoulder. "She rode in with us. She's over at the Reeves' place." I looked at Turk. "I'll fetch her, Turk. We'll meet you and Mister Wiggins over at the sheriff's office." I nodded to the yellow glow of lantern light illumining the sheriff's office.

Turk grunted. A sneer twisted his thin lips. His raspy voice was harsh. "I reckon you and them half-breeds' cockeyed idea about me and the boys rustling them forty head ain't worth two hoots and a holler now, huh, Bookbinder?" His cold eyes dared me to dispute him.

And the truth was, I couldn't. I still didn't trust him, but he had played me honest throughout the roundup. I grinned sheepishly. "I was wrong, Turk. Sheriff Turner told me I was, and I reckon he was right."

His sneer grew wider, and I knew then that the showdown between him and me was coming to a head. He yanked his pony around and dug his cruel spurs into the animal's flanks.

I went to fetch Miss Matilda, my feelings mixed. On the one hand, I was right pleased my obligation to my ex-poker partners was over. On the other, I was surprised to find I had enjoyed my stay at the Triple X despite Turk and his sullen compadres.

The Reeves' place was on the south edge of town. A white picket fence surrounded the neat clapboard house, and behind the fence raced a frantically barking dog, one of those long-haired brown and white sheepdogs.

Toby Reeves heard the racket and opened the door. "Hey, Barney. Shut up out there."

Immediately, the dog fell silent.

Toby waved me in. "Come on, Charley. He won't bother you now."

Nodding, I hurried onto the porch, keeping my eye on Barney. I wasn't crazy about the way he was eyeing me.

Miss Matilda and Beth were in the middle of freshening up, so Mrs. Reeves stuck me in the parlor and promptly poured me some tea in a tiny cup and scooted a platter of freshly baked sugar cookies across the table to me. "Help yourself, Mister Bookbinder. Matilda and Beth will be right out as soon as they rid themselves of the trail dust."

"Yes, Ma'am." I nodded briefly, looking for a place

for my battered and dirty hat. I ended up holding it in my lap. All the furniture in the parlor was too clean and fresh to lay my stained hat on. I even hated to sit on the furniture.

The parlor made me uncomfortable, for I recognized it as the kind a proper lady would like. For a few moments, my mind wandered, and I tried to imagine a fiddle-footed drifter like me with a fine woman like Miss Matilda in such a fancy room.

I grinned crookedly. She would fit in. I wouldn't. Me, I was better suited to dirt floors and log walls.

I sipped the tea. It was weak, but I reckoned that was what the gentry-folk preferred. Me, I'd take a cold beer or glass of whiskey anytime.

While I was waiting, Toby Reeves came in. "Charley. You did it. You sure as blazes did it," he exclaimed, striding across the floor with his hand outstretched. "You saved the town."

I started to rise, but he waved me back down, taking in the empty cup in front of me. "You need something stronger than Alice's tea," he said, laughing and reaching into a cabinet for a bottle of whiskey. He filled my cup and then chugged some from the bottle. "That's better, ain't it?"

"Sure is," I replied after draining my cup.

For the next few minutes, we made small talk, and then Miss Matilda swept into the room, dressed in a crisp blue gingham with a lacy white collar and cuffs. She wore a smile as wide as the Brazos River.

Awkwardly, I pushed to my feet, aware of the dust

billowing off my sweat-stained clothes. Just as I nodded to her, half a dozen gunshots echoed through the
dusk.

"What the . . ." Toby frowned at me.

A cold chill shot up my spine. I slapped my hat
back on my head and grabbed my six-gun. Cursing, I
burst from the parlor, racing up the dusty street toward
the sheriff's office where a crowd was already gathering.

"Let me through," I grunted, elbowing aside the curious citizens clustered in the door.

On the floor lay George Wiggins, blood pooling
around him, dripping through the cracks in the wooden
floor. Sheriff Turner sat in his chair, holding his leg.
He looked up when Toby and I skidded to a halt in
front of him.

With a grimace, he gestured to the back door. "It
was Turk. Him and his boys stole the money, and they
done killed Wiggins."

Chapter Twelve

The lantern light cast shadows about the room. Overhead, a thick gloom filled the loft. I looked around in time to see Toby Reeves push through the whispering crowd. I ran out the back door as Toby knelt by the cattle buyer.

The stars cast a bluish glow across the countryside. I paused, listening for the sound of hoofbeats, but the noise rolling out of the sheriff's office drowned any distant sounds.

Six-gun drawn, I sprinted north, straining over the thump of my own footsteps for some indication of the direction Turk had taken. Other than the sounds of the night, an owl hooting, a rabbit squealing, a coyote wailing, I heard nothing.

Mayor Markham stopped at my side, gasping for breath. "Anything?"

With a curse, I shook my head. "No." Reluctantly, I holstered my handgun and turned back to the jail. As soon as I saw about the sheriff, I planned to find Ben and Jim.

Back inside, I pushed through the crowd to the sheriff. Toby had cut the leg of the sheriff's trousers open, revealing a bloody red scar along the outside of the grizzled lawman's thigh. He clenched his teeth against the pain in his leg. "Find anything?"

"No." I nodded to his leg, noticing the powder burns where the slug tore through his jeans. "Is it bad?"

"Just a graze," said Toby. "The sheriff was lucky."

I glanced around at the townsfolk encircling the sheriff. Two men in suits stood in front, one tall and skinny, the other short and fat. Silas Henry and Ballister Fenton.

Miss Matilda stood next to the fat one, her arm around Beth's shoulder, her face drawn with dismay. She looked up at me.

I turned back to the sheriff. "What about the money? Turk get it?"

He dropped his head and nodded slowly. "Yeah. I came in and opened the safe. Turk pulled a gun on us and demanded the money. Wiggins tried to stop him. That's when they shot him. Closecut and Oklahoma Fats was right behind. They closed the door and started shooting. Turk grabbed the money, and the three of them hightailed it out the back door."

"Well, they're gone," I mumbled. "At least for tonight."

A soft sob caught my attention.

Beth was crying, and Miss Matilda was trying to soothe her.

Silas Henry and Ballister Fenton grinned at each other like two hogs that had just stumbled over a trough of rotten slop.

Ballister Fenton cleared his throat. In a sanctimonious voice, he said. "Very regretful, Miss Bledsoe. But, you understand, your note is—"

Ballister Fenton lost his voice when I jammed the muzzle of my six-gun in his nostril and growled. "Shut your mouth, Carpetbagger."

The muttering of the crowd faded away. I fought to control the anger twitching at my muscles. "She still has a few days before the mortgage is due. We don't need any sympathy from you or those like you. Understand?"

His thin face paled. He gulped, and his Adam's apple bobbed. "Y-yes sir."

Without taking my eyes off his, I muttered harshly, "Then git."

The two of them got.

After I left Miss Matilda and Beth at the Reeves' place, I rode into the night, searching for Jim and Ben Bledsoe. If anyone could find Turk, they could.

I found them camped three miles north of Sand Springs.

Ben glanced at Jim when I told them about Turk

and the others escaping. The older boy nodded. "We heard the shots."

"Yeah," Jim added. "We couldn't figure out what was going on."

I glanced up at the Big Dipper. Not yet midnight. I sighed and unsaddled Hardhead. "Reckon we can't do a thing until sunrise," I said as I tossed my gear by the small fire and staked my pony out to graze.

"Don't worry, Charley," said Ben. "We'll find them. Ain't nobody going to take my sister's ranch from her."

By the time the gray of dawn had burned off, we were heading southwest, searching the ground before us for sign. The three of us were spread in a half-mile skirmish line.

As usual, the night had been hot and dry, and sign didn't hold up for more than a few minutes before it started breaking down. Within hours, new tracks took on the appearance of ones two months old.

However, I hadn't counted on Ben's sharp eyes and keen tracking skills. Mid-morning, a gunshot broke the silence. In the distance, Ben waved us to him. We were due west of Sand Springs.

When we reached him, he was kneeling on the dusty ground, a puzzled frown on his face. He looked up, still puzzled. "These are new. The last eight, ten hours."

A grin leaped to my face, but disappeared quickly

when he added. "But, there are only two sets of tracks."

Instantly, I had the answer. "That means they split up. Odds are, those two are Closecut's and Fat's. Turk went another direction, but they're all planning on meeting somewhere. Turk is probably carrying the money."

The boys considered my theory.

Both boys nodded. Jim spoke up. "How can we be sure Turk will keep his word and meet these two?"

"Yeah," said Ben. "And knowing Turk, I figure he'll doublecross them." He nodded to the tracks in the sand before us.

Their arguments made sense. "Okay. You two follow this trail. I'll backtrack until I find where Turk broke away. If we don't meet up by mid-afternoon, then let's meet. . . ." I looked around. In the distance, I spotted the top of the escarpment peeking over the horizon back to the north. "Let's meet at the cave entrance tonight. Then we can look at what we have and decide what we need to do."

We parted, the boys heading west, me heading east along the trail back toward town. The sign was easy to follow. I kept waiting to run across the third set of tracks. Chances were, after they bolted from the jail, they hung together for a couple miles and then split.

After two hours, I spotted Sand Springs on the horizon, but still I backtracked over only two sets of hoof prints. When I was still an hour from Sand Springs, I began to wonder. Could the three have split as soon as they burst from jail?

Suddenly, my pony stiffened. His ears perked forward, and he peered back to the southeast. I followed his gaze. A dark object blurred into the horizon. I studied it, but it did not appear to be moving.

Hardhead seemed mighty curious. He shook his head and snorted. Curious myself, I pressed my left knee into his side, guiding him back toward the object.

After a few minutes, the object moved, and I made out the shape of a horse. I chuckled. There were no wild ponies around, so someone's animal must have wandered off. As I drew closer, I made out a saddle on the dun's back. Instantly, I became wary, shucking my six-gun and scanning the grassy prairie carefully.

The dun whinnied nervously as we approached. "What the blazes," I muttered, recognizing Turk's dun, a yellowish brown cow horse with dark stockings, mane, and tail. The reins were wrapped around the saddle horn.

Quickly, I looked around, expecting to see the brawny foreman sprawled on the ground, but I found nothing. "Easy, boy, easy," I muttered, edging my bay forward until I could pluck the reins from around the saddle horn. "Where's your owner, boy?" I whispered, continuing to search the flat countryside even as I was dallying the reins to my own saddle horn.

Slowly, I picked my way over the dun's back trail. With each step, my frown grew deeper and the questions tumbling through my head became more puzzling. From the sign, the animal had been grazing, drifting slowly. After about a mile, I came across a small patch of disturbed soil where the dun had milled about.

Beyond, the tracks indicated the pony had been galloping. I reined Hardhead up, pausing to stare over the prairie at the small town some half-mile distant. I couldn't believe what the sign was saying.

Maybe I'd find some trace of Turk within the next few hundred yards. Maybe one of the sheriff's slugs had found its mark. Could be Turk had been knocked from the saddle, spooking the horse.

But, if that was so, where was Turk?

There was no place to hide on the prairie other than beneath sagebrush or buffalo grass, none of which would hide a man of Turk's bulk.

On the outskirts of Sand Springs, a few dark figures paused at the river's edge, peering in my direction. There was a stirring of activity. Two or three of the figures darted into the sheriff's office.

The activity didn't bother me. Nor did I suspect anything when I saw a small figure astride a large white horse racing across the shallow river and turning in my direction. Pulling Turk's cow horse after me, I continued in a trot to town.

Then I recognized the small rider on the white horse. Beth!

She leaned low over the animal's neck, urging him faster and faster. Her long black hair whipped out behind her. When she drew closer, I saw she was riding bareback with no bridle.

I reined up, grinning at her. She was some horsewoman.

She waved me back. "Go back, Mister Bookbinder. Back. Run!"

Hardhead stutter-stepped nervously as she slid the white pony to a halt. "What's going on?" I said, noticing several ponies with mounted riders splashing across the river.

Beth threw a frightened glance over her shoulder. "Run! Fast!"

"But, but why? What the blazes. . . ."

She interrupted. "It's the posse. They think you doublecrossed Matilda and helped kill the cattle buyer. They want to hang you."

Chapter Thirteen

I stared at Beth in disbelief. The baking July sun drew heat waves from the earth, distorting the oncoming riders like images from a bad dream. For a moment, I felt as if I were standing to the side watching all the action unfold in slow motion.

Beth pulled the white around and dug her heels into its flanks. She rammed her pony into mine. "Run," she yelled once again as the big horse beneath her leaped forward into a gallop at right angles to the oncoming posse.

I sat frozen in my saddle like one of those store window dummies until the first rifle shot. The slug whining past my head got my attention. I threw Turk's reins from my saddlehorn and yanked Hardhead around. Within three steps, he was at a full gallop, racing away from Beth.

119

Now what was going on? I'd ridden out last night on the side of the law, and this morning, that same law wanted to hang me. What the blazes had taken place while I was gone?

Leaning low, I stroked Hardhead's neck. "Faster, boy, faster," I whispered, knowing there were only one or two animals in Texas that could catch us, and none of them were in the posse behind. Hardhead was so fast he could turn on a quarter and give you fifteen cents change.

I headed east, across the river, and began a wide swing back to the north, hoping to out-distance the posse by the time I reached the *Diablo Paisaje*. If not, I'd have to lose them in the primitive wilderness before ducking into the cave.

Within half an hour, the posse had dropped below the horizon. I didn't know if those old boys were still following or had given up the pursuit. Either way, I wasn't taking a chance.

I had never ridden this far east in this country before, but using the sun, I made a fair guess at where the *Diablo Paisaje* was located. I cut back to the northwest.

The whole mess back at Sand Springs was too bizarre to figure. What the Sam Hill could have happened to make the sheriff and the town believe I had anything at all to do with murdering George Wiggins and stealing the twenty thousand dollars?

When the shooting occurred, I was at the Reeves'

place picking up Miss Matilda, so no one could have accused me of taking an active part in the murder. The only answer I could see was that for some reason, the town believed I had planned the whole scheme with Turk.

I started searching for explanations. If I'd been part of the plan, would I have ridden back into town pulling Turk's cow horse? Couldn't someone in town understand that? Of course, Turk could have stolen another pony. And his dun could have spooked and grazed out to where I found him.

I shook my head. Several pieces of the puzzle were missing. I had a lot of legwork ahead of me to discover those pieces. Maybe once I found them, I'd find the truth behind the murder of George Wiggins, retrieve the stolen money, and save Miss Matilda's ranch.

I reached the south side of *Diablo Paisaje* just before sunset. The reddish-orange glow of the sun lit the empty prairie behind me. I rode a couple miles east along the edge of the forest of boulders and trees before cutting due north, staying on little-traveled deer trails, all the while gradually working toward the limestone escarpment.

Jim and Ben were waiting just inside the cave entrance. "We see you come," Ben said, looking up at me.

In the shadows of the cave, their outlines blurred, but their white teeth shone out clearly. "What about Fats and Closecut?"

"They ride into Buffalo Wallow," Ben said, nodding to the west.

Buffalo Wallow was no more than a greasy spot on the trail several miles west of Sand Springs, a meeting place for rawhiders, rustlers, and robbers. When I rode through the shanty town a few weeks earlier, I pulled up to the saloon, looked around, then rode on out, wanting nothing at all to do with the town. The next day, I rode into Sand Springs.

"What about Turk? The boys meet up with him?"

"No." Jim shook his head. "We follow two sets of tracks into town. They stop at the saloon."

"The two, they met up with no one," added Ben.

"Turk might have already been inside."

The boys grinned at each other, and I knew they had checked on that possibility. "No," said Jim. "He not inside."

Ben laid his hand on Hardhead's muzzle briefly. "Come. There is venison and coffee." He paused, glanced at Jim. "Give him your rope." He went on to explain. "We will be climbing up into the mountain. There is no light in the tunnel. You must hold to the rope. The tunnel forks into dropoffs without bottom."

I caught my breath. "Dropoffs? Then . . . then how do you know which tunnel to take?"

He replied casually. "I have been here many times. Just hold to Jim's rope and lead your horse. You will be safe."

With bottomless holes around, I figured I would do exactly what he suggested, so, dismounting, I grabbed the rope and led Hardhead after them. "We must talk while we eat," I said to the darkness ahead of me. "A lot has happened. Things we never expected."

The tunnel could not have been any darker if I'd closed my eyes. As I followed them upward, I remembered the strange tracks and the curious sounds upon my first visit to the *Paisaje*. "A week or so ago when I was poking around up here, I ran across animal tracks like I had never seen. You boys ever see them?"

For several seconds, neither boy answered, but I had the distinct feeling that my question had shocked them. Ben finally replied. "The tracks you speak of. Like a square rock?"

"Yeah. I'd say so. And then I noticed a smell worse than a skunk. Almost rotten."

A few seconds elapsed before either boy replied. This time, Jim spoke. "We have only seen its sign. Not the creature itself."

Shivers ran up my spine. I glanced over my shoulder, my imagination conjuring the creature in the dark tunnel behind me. I tried to keep my voice from quivering. "Any idea what it is?"

Jim giggled.

Ben silenced him. "He laughs because I believe it is Spirit of the *Mistai*. But, he is still a child."

"Mistai?"

Ben hesitated, searching for the right words. "Something like what white people call ghosts. I have seen huge trees it has destroyed, great boulders it has thrown about like tiny rocks."

Jim chortled. "Yes. Ghosts with the bodies of animals and heads of people."

My imagination summoned up all sorts of twisted and ferocious images. "So, you've never seen this thing, huh?"

Ben's voice was somber. "No. But it does live here in the *Paisaje*. We leave food for it so it will think well of us."

I fell silent, listening behind us for any sign of following footsteps. Finally, we halted. I sensed the tunnel had broadened.

We stopped. In the next instant, a spark punched a hole in the darkness. Seconds later, a small fire pushed away the shadows, revealing a large room, the one we had been in a few days earlier.

I looked around. "What about smoke from the fire? Can't someone smell it?"

Jim gestured upward. "I told you before. There are many passages. When the smoke reaches outside, no one can tell where it came from."

While we ate, I told them all that had happened, from finding Turk's horse to the chase by the posse.

"What of Matilda and Beth?" Ben leaned forward, his slender face tight with concern.

"I imagine they are still at the Reeves'."

"Did the posse see Beth warn you?"

"I don't see how they couldn't keep from it. We were out in plain sight."

The boys exchanged alarmed looks. Suddenly, I understood. "You think the town will take it out on them? Matilda is white, like the town."

A sneer twisted Jim's thin lips. "But she is an 'Indian Lover'. That is all the white man thinks."

I stared at them, skeptical.

The dancing flames cast shadows over their dark and serious faces like warpaint. "We should speak to Matilda and Beth," Ben opined.

Slowly, I nodded. "Then maybe we'd best go into town and see that they're all right. Bring them back here."

Crooked smiles broke the sober grimaces on their faces. Ben grunted. "I believe you are a good man, Charley Bookbinder. I think our father would have liked you."

"So do I," Jim chimed in.

I grinned sheepishly. A loner like me was hard put to come by compliments. "Thanks, boys."

We rode through the *Diablo Paisaje* without incident.

During the ride back to Sand Springs, I tried to put my ideas in some kind of order. There had only been two sets of tracks the morning after the murder. They led to the saloon in Buffalo Wallow. Where had Turk and the twenty thousand dollars disappeared? Had he stolen a horse and headed in a different direction?

That was the only answer that made sense.

Just this morning, the boys and I had begun our western swing from north of Sand Springs. We ran across Closecut and Oklahoma Fat's sign about five miles west of the small town. From there, I headed east along the back trail, searching for the spot where Turk had broken off.

Chances are, if I hadn't been chased by the posse, I might have cut his sign back to the south and east. I figured that would come tomorrow.

We skirted Sand Springs, and when we spotted the lights of Toby Reeves' place, I called the boys. "Hold it here."

They pulled their ponies up close to mine. "The one chance we have of proving I had nothing to do with the murder is to run Turk down. Now, I figure he headed out south or east. One of you boys will have to take Miss Matilda and Beth back to the caves." I paused. "I've got to find Turk's trail tomorrow."

Ben whispered softly, "Jim will take them. I will stay with you."

Jim hesitated, then nodded briefly.

Even in the soft glow of the starlight, I read the determination on Ben's face. "Good. The two of us," I added, "will cut Turk's sign tomorrow. When we find him, we'll bring him back to the caves with the money. Then we'll worry about how we prove I had nothing to do with Wiggins's murder."

"Let's go," Ben said, reining his horse around.

"Hold on," I called out. "Reeves has a dog that barks at everything. I don't know if he bites or not, but he barks."

In the starlight, I saw Jim grin. Ben explained.

"Don't worry, Mister Bookbinder. Jim can talk a robin down from its nest."

I was skeptical, and when Jim slipped off his pony and disappeared into the night in the direction of the lighted windows, I kept expecting frenzied barking to shatter the silence of the night.

Not even the crickets stopped chirruping.

Finally, there came a soft whistle. Ben grinned. "Let's go, Charley."

The brown- and white-haired sheepdog was wagging his tail and licking at Jim's hand when we rode up. I shook my head in amazement. The younger boy put his finger over his lips and pointed to the front of the house. "A man is guarding the house. I do not know who he is."

Shucking my six-gun, I motioned for them to remain here with each other. I slipped to the corner of the clapboard house, then stepped into the shadows along the side. Slowly, I eased down into a crouch and peered toward the front of the house, searching the shadows ahead.

The last play I wanted was gunfire. I didn't want to come out of this mess a killer. I strained for the slightest sound. Only the gentle summer breeze. In the distance, an owl hooted. Back to the north, in the direction of the *Diablo Paisaje*, a coyote howled.

A boot scraped on the hardpan. I froze. Moments later, the yellow flare of a striking match glowed from around the corner.

Tiptoeing forward, I picked up a handful of dirt and rocks and grinned to myself. As I drew closer, I could hear the guard breathing, the ragged, struggling breathing of an older man.

Dropping to one knee, I peered around the corner. He stood about three feet from me, leaning back with one boot propped against the side of the house.

The tip of his cigarette glowed. When the glow faded, I tossed the rocks and dirt beyond him.

"What the—" He spun, grabbing for his handgun.

I jammed the muzzle of my Colt in his back. "Don't move. Don't say a word." He stiffened. "Down on your belly," I growled.

He did as I ordered. Quickly, I used his belt to tie his hands, his neckerchief to keep him from shouting, and his vest to snug down his feet. I placed the muzzle of my handgun to the back of his head.

"One of my men will be watching from the corner. You make a sound, any sound in the next ten minutes, and you'll be swinging a wide loop for St. Peter. You hear?"

The man nodded hurriedly.

I slipped back to the boys. Jim pointed to a darkened window. "That is where they sleep."

I didn't even ask him how he knew. If he said that was their bedroom, I wasn't about to question him.

Gently, I tapped on the window.

Moments later, a face appeared. Miss Matilda. She frowned, but quickly opened the window. Before I could speak, she laid her finger on her lips, then nodded over her shoulder. Silent as a small kitten on a rug, she disappeared back into the room for only an instant, then returned with Beth. Without a sound, they slipped from the window and swung up on the boys' ponies.

Moving silently across the yard, we exited through the gate. Jim knelt by the sheepdog, scrubbed his ears, then closed the gate. He climbed up in the saddle.

Three hundred yards from the house, we pulled up. I spoke in a whisper. "Jim, you and Ben take them back to the caves."

Ben protested. "I go with you."

"You can't. We didn't think about it, but you need both horses to get the women back to the caves."

For a moment, I thought the young man would argue, but he had grown up understanding the reality of a Westerner's life. Sometimes it's smarter to pull your freight than your gun.

Matilda spoke up. "What happened to the guard outside the house?"

I told her. "He's fine. Just tied up like a maverick."

"Then you be careful, Charley. The whole town is looking for you. That's why the guard was there."

"Why?"

"They think you and Turk were in on the murder of George Wiggins together."

Just like I thought. I shook my head and reached over and laid my hand on hers. I felt a tingle. "Don't worry," I said. "I'll be fine."

Chapter Fourteen

Not wanting to miss Turk's sign, I rode north to the camp the boys had made the night before. The night before? It seemed like a month ago that we had ridden from the camp, cutting Closecut's and Oklahoma Fats' sign several miles west of Sand Springs.

I figured that if I rode to their camp, then made a swing east and south around Sand Springs until I reached the two jaspers' original trail on the west, I would run across Turk's sign.

So I rose early and struck out, knowing I had to keep an extra keen eye on the ground. Almost thirty-six hours had passed since Turk and his boys had hightailed it out of town. The steady wind, the dusty ground, both lent themselves to obscuring sign.

I kept Sand Springs just below the horizon on my

right as I rode. I found sign, but most of it was older than what I was looking for.

By the time I reached the river on the south side of town, the sun was directly overhead. I studied the riverbanks, up and down for about a mile on either side, but ran across no new sign.

Studying my backtrail, I muttered a curse. I had covered the east and south side of town with no luck at all. No sign of Turk or the money. Oklahoma Fats' and Closecut's trail was only a few miles distant farther west.

I felt as if I had a lead weight in my stomach. A tiny worry was beginning to nag at me. Would I ever find Turk? Had I been the burly foreman, I would have stayed close to the river, but the boys and I had found no sign north of town along the river banks, and I had found none on the river banks south of Sand Springs.

I paused in the river and let Hardhead drink while I splashed the icy water on my face and head. I stared back to the west, across the flat, open prairie beneath a washed-out blue sky. What if I didn't find his sign?

But it had to be there. People didn't just vanish. The only way any hombre could get out of town without leaving sign was by flying like the birds. And flying like birds would never come about. Not in my lifetime.

Swinging back into the saddle, I headed out, with each step the weight in my stomach growing heavier.

I fought against the growing conviction that I wouldn't find a trace of Turk.

Two or three times throughout the afternoon, I spotted travelers in the distance. Each time, I swung down and pulled Hardhead down on the ground beside me. I wasn't anxious to run into a posse nor have a stranger carry word of me back into Sand Springs.

I reached the western trail at sunset with no luck. I pulled up and stared over my backtrail, trying to put together some logical explanation for not finding any sign of Turk. Idly, I pulled out my bag of Bull Durham and rolled a cigarette.

After twisting the ends tightly, I stuck the cigarette between my lips and reached for a match. For years, I had struck matches by holding the stem in the fingers of one hand and snapping the head with my thumbnail.

This time, part of the head broke off and fell on the thigh of my faded jeans. Quickly, I brushed it away, but not before the small fire had scorched a tiny spot on my trousers. "One of these days you'll burn yourself up, Charley," I muttered, taking a deep drag on the cigarette and reining Hardhead back north toward the escarpment.

I had a heap of thinking to do, but if someone had told me that at that moment I had all the answers I needed to solve the entire mess, I would have called them a liar.

Chapter Fifteen

Clouds rolled across the starry sky before I reached *Diablo Paisaje*. All I could make out as I approached the primal country was a darker line where the forest of rugged boulders and twisted trees met the prairie. Abruptly, Hardhead stiffened and whinnied. His ears perked forward as he snorted just like that day on my first visit to the *Paisaje* when I saw the unknown tracks and heard the strange sounds.

I hesitated, my hand resting on the butt of my Army Colt. I stared at the ominous wall of darkness ahead of me. I had a general idea in which direction lay the escarpment, but I wasn't looking forward to feeling my way along the narrow trails, especially with that unknown creature out there.

Jim had scoffed at Ben's notion of the thing being a ghost, but Jim was young. He'd been in the white man's world half his life, so much of the Indians' superstitions were lost on him.

Ben was a different drink of water. From what little I had learned among the Shawnee, mystical attributes were given to physical creatures. And often, the two beliefs fused, becoming a creature exalted and feared.

I took a deep breath in an effort to slow my breathing. I ran my tongue over my dry lips and peered into the night. Slowly, I reached for my handgun.

Then, a soft whistle from the darkness to my left caught my attention. I peered into the gloom, and then a shadowy figure materialized from the darkness and headed toward me.

As he drew closer, I recognized Jim by the way he rode in the saddle. "Jim? That you?"

His voice drifted back through the night. "Yes. It's me, Mister Bookbinder. Ben sent me out to bring you back. Miss Matilda is waiting."

I sagged back in my saddle in relief.

Ten minutes later, we were all squatted around the small fire. I put myself around some broiled venison and Arbuckle's coffee while telling them of the futility of my search. "I moved slow. I found Turk and Closecut's first sign, and the posse sign. I didn't miss a thing." I looked at each of them. "From the sign, I'd give hundred to one odds that Turk Warner is still in Sand Springs."

Miss Matilda shook her head. "But he can't be.

Everyone in town was looking for him and you. They searched all the buildings and homes on the chance that one of you might have doubled back and hidden."

Beth spoke up. "Ben, you and Jim said you found the other two over in Buffalo Wallow. Why don't you tell Sheriff Turner about them. Let him arrest them. They'll know where Turk is."

Her question made sense to me, but Miss Matilda interrupted. "Buffalo Wallow isn't in the sheriff's jurisdiction, Beth. He can't go over there without the proper authority."

The small, dark-complexioned girl frowned up at Matilda. "I don't understand." She turned to me. "Is that right, Mister Bookbinder?"

A flush of embarrassment burned my cheeks. I'd forgotten about jurisdiction. "Yeah. That's right. You see, Beth, sheriffs are elected by a county. Their authority is good only in that county. Obviously, Buffalo Wallow is in another county which means that Sheriff Turner can't arrest Oklahoma Fats or Closecut."

Jim piped up. "But what if they did come back here. Sheriff Turner could arrest them then, couldn't he?"

Matilda and I exchanged looks. I shrugged. "Yeah. I reckon he could. Don't you?" I arched an eyebrow at her.

She nodded. "Yes."

For several long moments, we sat staring into the fire.

I cleared my throat. "Well, folks. I think I'm going

to take me a nap until sunrise and then head over to Buffalo Wallow. I'm going to see if I can persuade Fats or Closecut to come back to Sand Springs."

A round of grins greeted my announcement.

Two minutes later, we were all sprawled around the fire, blankets up about our necks. I dropped off quickly, but something during the early morning hours awakened me. I lay motionless, staring into the darkness above my head.

Suddenly, a rotten, putrefied odor swept through the large room, lasting only seconds before it vanished upon the next random breeze.

I pulled my six-gun from the holster and, gripping it in my hand, lay it on my chest under the blanket. And I waited.

Every sound was magnified.

Sleep didn't come for the rest of the night.

Next morning before we parted, I had Jim and Ben promise that once they got the back to the ranch, they would remain there to look after Miss Matilda and Beth.

Ben wanted to ride to Buffalo Wallow with me.

"There's no time to wait," I explained to Ben. "It'll take you four hours to the ranch and back. As far as we know, those two might have already lit a shuck out of Buffalo Wallow. If they did, I'll follow. Besides, you're needed here more. Look after Miss Matilda and Beth. I'll be back. That I guarantee."

Reluctantly, they agreed.

As we parted outside the cave, Miss Matilda laid her hand on my arm. "Be careful, Charley. You hear?"

I saw the concern in her dark brown eyes. I tried to give her a casual, devil-may-care grin. "Don't worry. I'm always careful. If I'm not back by morning, that means I'm trailing Fats and Closecut."

Her face remained solemn. "Just take care."

I swore to myself I would.

I had ridden less than five minutes when a sudden thought struck me. I reined Hardhead around, but the four of them had already disappeared deep into the *Paisaje*. I muttered a curse under my breath. Just in case there were problems at the ranch, we should have set up some kind of signal, a lamp, a gate down, something that would serve as a warning.

With a resigned sigh, I reined about and rode on.

Buffalo Wallow lived up to its name. The town was even more reprehensible and repugnant than the mud hole after which it was named.

The shantytown was made up of buffalo hide tents, *jacales* with gaps in the wall wide enough for dogs to run, and ramshackle sheds of weathered planks. The only structure that appeared capable of standing up to a sneeze was the saloon, an adobe structure with low doors and ceilings. As with the other buildings, only rawhide or pieces of dirty gingham covered the windows.

Two shad-bellied horses stood hipshot at the hitching rail, a white with albino eyes and a paint hanging its head. I tied Hardhead at the end of the rail, not anxious for him to catch whatever they appeared to have.

I paused and fished the two half eagles from my boots, my emergency fund.

Inside, a fat bartender with an even larger wife leered at me from behind the bar. "What'll it be, Stranger?"

Two rail-thin hombres sat hunched over a table at the rear, one tall, the other short. They looked around, their beady eyes taking me in.

I dropped a coin on the rough bar. "Whiskey."

With practiced moves, the barkeep swept up the coin, deposited it in his pocket, slapped down a tumbler, and poured a generous drink. "There you go, stranger. That'll cut the dust, sure thing."

I gulped it down. That whiskey was so raw that it would have cut through a plate of iron. It burned and scraped all the way to my belly. I shivered.

He tilted the bottle. "Another?"

I waved him away, at the same time tossing another coin on the bar. "I'm looking for two hombres who come through here a couple days back. Tall skinny one, big fat one. Go by the handles of Closecut and Oklahoma Fats. I wrangled with them over at the Triple X south of Sand Springs."

He hesitated, but his greedy eyes kept going back to the shiny coin on the bar.

Behind me came the scrape of chair legs against the floor, then footsteps. I glanced in the dirty mirror to see the two thin cowpokes amble out. Moments later, the sound of retreating hoof beats echoed through the open door.

"It was like this," I said, prodding the barkeeper. "I was out on the range when they left. Heard they quit for a cattle drive heading to Wichita. I got a hankering to do some traveling, so I figured I'd run them down and see if I could get in on the deal."

I must have looked dumb as a skunk to him, for he leaned forward and laid his hand on the coin. He whispered. "They was here. Rode out yesterday. Took the San Antone road." He paused and grinned, revealing a set of rotting teeth. "Don't reckon they gone far. They took six bottles of whiskey with them. The two of 'em, they struck me to be the kind not to let whiskey age too long in the bottle."

He poured me another shot of rotgut. "Have one for the road. It's a mighty long piece to the next watering hole."

I choked it down, just to be hospitable, nodded, and hurried outside to my horse where I gulped half a canteen of warm water, a much more satisfying drink than the shot of whiskey.

Swinging into the saddle, I headed west, shaking my head to clear the whiskey cobwebs. I was beginning to wonder if Fats and Closecut had anything at all to do with the murder. For cowpokes on the run, they were sure taking their time.

Outside of town, I noticed a faint cloud of dust hanging over the road. A warning sign went up in the back of my head.

Those two cowpokes back in the saloon. Were they heading somewhere in particular or waiting for me? I took no chances. The country through which we were passing was a mixture of open plains and rolling hills covered with bluestem and switchgrass. At the base of the hills grew stands of live oak and shin oak along the wet-weather watercourses, ideal spots for bushwhackers.

I pulled a couple hundred yards off the narrow trail. If those two hombres were waiting to bushwhack me, I hoped they would be paying more attention to the road than their backs.

The problem with underestimating your enemy is that by the time you find out you miscalculated, it's usually too late.

The thick growth at the base of the hills was a logical spot for ambush. My mistake was paying too much attention to the obvious sites for an ambush and not enough to those in plain sight.

I pulled up just below the crest of a hill and peered down into the valley below. The winding trail twisted through a thick stand of oaks. Off to my right, halfway down the slope, was a shinnery patch, a thick growth of stunted oaks the size of a man's wrist stretching about ten or twelve feet high.

Ever since I left Buffalo Wallow, my nerves had been on edge. The last few minutes, they had grown even tighter. Somewhere out there, ahead of me, the two cowpokes waited. I flexed my fingers, tapping them against the worn-shiny pecan wood handle of my Army Colt.

I kept my eyes moving, searching the countryside around me, but focusing on the narrow road. Sweat stung my eyes. I removed my hat and dragged my sleeve across my forehead.

That's when the rattlesnake saved my life.

Chapter Sixteen

From beneath a thick patch of switchgrass, a lightning-fast blur shot out at Hardhead's hoof. The startled bay whinnied and spun, almost jerking me out of the saddle.

At the same time, a rifle boomed, and my hat went flying.

I tightened my legs about the bay's belly, grabbed for the saddlehorn, and shucked my six-gun, all the while spinning and sunfishing like a whirling top.

I started pulling the trigger, aiming blindly in the direction the shot came from.

Hardhead spun a couple more times, then started crowhopping across the side of the hill. I looked up and we were heading straight for two astonished cowpokes. I threw up my Colt and fired.

One jasper threw up his hands and somersaulted

backward off his pony. The other one spun and dug his big-roweled spurs into his cowhorse.

Hardhead grabbed the bit in his teeth and took after the fleeing cowboy. I yanked on the reins. "Whoa, boy. Whoa." But he kept going. I don't know if he was scared or just mad, or a combination of both.

I tugged and yelled. "Blast you, whoa, you ornery churn-headed piece of buzzard bait. Whoa!"

After a short distance, he veered off and began to slow. Then he made his mistake and opened his mouth. I popped the bit back against his gums. He slowed then, real fast.

Off to the north, a cloud of dust marked the frantic retreat of the remaining bushwhacker. I looked back up the hill at the other who lay motionless on the ground. He was the smaller of the two.

I reloaded my Colt, holstered it, and shucked the Winchester 66 from the boot. I was a better shot with a rifle than a handgun.

I rode to within about fifty yards, then placed a slug in the sand about ten yards from his head. He threw up a hand and waved for me to stop.

"Throw away your gun," I yelled.

"Don't have it."

I placed another slug about five yards from his head. In the next moment, a handgun flew through the air. Levering another cartridge into the chamber, I rode closer.

He struggled to sit up. Blood soaked his left shoulder. From where I sat, I figured I hit him just below the collarbone. He glared up at me, his bearded face grimacing in pain. "Now, why'd you have to go and shoot me like that?"

I stared at him in disbelief.

He managed to stumble to his feet, all the while cradling his left arm to his belly. He was no taller than a youngster.

I couldn't believe I was sitting here arguing with some scrawny jasper over who should have shot who. "What are you talking about, Mister? You shot at me first."

"Not me. It was Pete."

"Well, that don't really make me no never mind seeing as he's your partner. You old boys shot at me first."

"Yeah, but we wasn't going to hurt nobody. All we was going to do was rob you. We ain't killers or nothing. That's how we make our living, robbing old boys like you." He glanced down at the bleeding hole in his shoulder. "Now, you messed up everything. You ruined my shirt. I gotta pay the Doc to patch me up. My horse is run away, and I ain't going to be able to work 'til my shoulder is healed up."

He had me flabbergasted. Here someone had taken a shot at me, and now he wanted me to feel guilty. I shook my head and cocked the Winchester. His eyes grew wide. I cleared my throat. "Now, you listen here, Mister. Robbing folks is almost as bad as killing them. You better thank your lucky stars I'm letting you go.

By all rights, I oughta take your boots and make you walk back to town."

He screwed his face up into a frown. "But I'm bleeding."

"Yeah, but you ain't dying."

Standing there, slump-shouldered, teary-eyed, and whining, he was a pitiful sight. I shook my head at my own lunacy. "Okay. I'll bring your pony to you, but that's it."

Tears rolled down his thin cheeks, cutting paths in the grime caked on the cowpoke. "You're a true saint, Mister. I'm right glad Pete and me didn't rob you. And if any of your compadres ever ride through here, you just tell them to say that 'they're friends of Pete Darcy and Big Al Harger.' " He jabbed himself in the chest with his thumb. "That's me. Big Al."

Big Al? Not five feet tall and Big Al?

I eyed him carefully. Maybe God did have a sense of humor. Tilting the muzzle until it pointed right at the middle of his chest, I said, "I'm bringing your pony, Al. But if this is some kind of trick, I ain't even going to take time to bury you."

He shook his head emphatically. "Honest, Mister. I ain't lying." He laid his hand on his shoulder. "I got to get the doc to look at this. It's bleeding something fierce."

I pointed to my neck. "See that little piece of cloth on your neck?"

"My bandanna? Yeah. Why?"

"You might consider taking it off and packing it

against the hole. That'll help the bleeding, and maybe you'll live 'til you get back into Buffalo Wallow."

He stared at me several seconds, clearly puzzled. Then, a flash of understanding lit his eyes. "Yeah. Yeah, that'll work just fine."

While Big Al tended the hole in his shoulder, I rounded up his pony.

He clambered into the saddle.

I stopped him before he rode off. "I come here looking for two men. They came into town a couple days back. A fat one and a skinny one. You see'm?"

For a moment, he hesitated, his eyes growing devious.

"You better tell me the truth, Big Al, or I'll kick you off that horse and take your boots."

He nodded quickly. "Yeah. Yeah. We seen them. We was going to rob them, but Miss Rose wouldn't let us in the house."

I blinked. I had missed something. "Miss Rose?"

"Yeah. She owns the house up in Limestone Hill."

"House?"

"Yeah. You know, one that . . . ah, well, one of them houses you never would tell your Ma about. Well, Pete and me followed the two cowpokes there. We was going inside to rob them, but Miss Rose wouldn't let us in because we didn't have ten dollars."

"Ten dollars? What for?"

"Why, that's what it cost to go in her house."

I couldn't believe my ears. "Did you ever consider just sneaking into the house?"

He stared at me in disbelief. "No. Miss Rose wouldn't like that. It wouldn't be honest."

"Why didn't you wait for them outside?"

He pondered the question a moment, then grinned sheepishly. "You know, I don't reckon we thought of that."

I couldn't help chuckling. "Tell me, Al. How much do you and Pete make at this robbing business?"

He shifted around in his saddle uneasily. "Well, not much, I don't reckon, but it's all we know. Handed down to both of us from our old men. Sort of what you might call a family tradition."

I sat back in the saddle and shook my head. "Well, Al, you do what you want. But, if you want my advice, you and Pete best take up another line of work. You hear?"

I reached Limestone Hill just before dark. Miss Rose's establishment wasn't hard to spot, it having the sign, ROSE, painted in garish greenish-yellow letters four feet high across the front of the clapboard building. Next to it sat an unsteady structure of weathered planks and boards that claimed to be the general store and livery. Next to it, butting up against the Limestone Hill for which the town was named was the saloon, nothing more than a ragged, three-sided canvas tent, the front of which was wide open.

But I didn't need to enter the wicked doors of Rose's Emporium, for I spotted Oklahoma Fats and Closecut next door in the saloon, bellying up to the bar, which was a crooked plank stretched between two whiskey barrels.

I slipped the loop off the hammer of my Colt, uncertain just what kind of greeting the boys would give me. I had no idea how much or how little they knew about the events of the last few days. If they knew a heap, then I had to figure out how to get them back to Sand Springs. But, somehow, I had the feeling they were just as much in the dark about Turk as I was.

Closecut looked around as I was tying Hardhead to the corner post of the tent. A sneer curled his lips and twisted his bearded face. He elbowed Oklahoma Fats.

I dropped my hands to my sides, noting they made no move toward their sidearms. Maybe I was right. Maybe they didn't know any more than I did.

Closecut took a step toward me. "I reckon I'm surprised to see you, Charley."

"Well, it don't go double, Closecut. I been looking for you boys . . . you and Turk."

They exchanged puzzled looks. Fats waddled up beside his skinny partner. "What do you mean about Turk?"

"Just what I said, I reckon." I glanced around the saloon. "He around?"

A frown knit Closecut's dirty forehead. "No, he ain't. We been waiting here for him."

"Yeah. He shoulda been here a couple days back."

Closecut jabbed his elbow in his partner's ample belly. He eyed me warily. "What you asking all the questions for, huh, Charley?"

Suddenly, I knew that Turk had snookered them; that he'd sent them in one direction, and he headed the other with the money, all twenty thousand dollars. "Well, I'll tell you, boys. If you didn't know it, your partner stole the cattle money, killed George Wiggins, and disappeared a couple days back. About the time you rode out of Sand Springs."

Oklahoma Fats' eyes bugged out. He spun on Closecut. "Did you hear what—"

"Shut up!" Closecut interrupted. "Don't say nothing."

"Look, boys. I ain't here after you or for the law or nothing. You boys pulled off a nice little job. Of course, it left me in trouble with the law, so I figured I was rightfully entitled to a cut." I made a show of glancing around and then rolling my eyes. "But, I reckon if Turk was going to cut you in, he would have already been here since he hightailed out of town just after you old boys."

Closecut stuck his nose in my face. "Look here, boy. You telling the gospel truth?"

I decided to take a chance. I held up my hand. "I swear. After all, I knew about you fellers rustling a few Triple X head here and there, but I never said nothing. I always figured one hand washes the other, you know what I mean?"

Oklahoma Fats nodded his head like a happy puppy dog. "Yeah, but we ain't seen Turk. He come out of the sheriff's office where he'd been rubbing shoulders with that cattle buyer and told us he'd meet us in Buffalo Waller. If he didn't show up in Buffalo Waller, we was to come here."

I looked at Closecut. The angular cowpoke nodded. "You didn't hear any gunshots?"

"Nope. He told us to ride out, and that's what we did."

"And you haven't seen him, huh?"

Closecut growled. "You mean, he ain't still in Sand Springs?"

"Nope." I shook my head. "Like I said, there was a killing, but by the time we got to the sheriff's office, Turk and you boys was gone. Everybody figured you was all in it together. Why, I wouldn't be surprised if old Sheriff Turner didn't have warrants out on you two fellers already."

"Warrants?" Closecut dropped his hand to the butt of his six-gun. "You thinking on collecting?"

"Not me." I held up my hand. "He figures I helped you boys plan it. He's after me too. That's why I figured I deserved a cut."

Oklahoma Fats muttered a few curses. "Well, you ain't getting no cuts from me 'cause I ain't got nothing to give a cut from."

"Me neither." Closecut hissed. "Blast that Turk."

I studied the two for several more seconds, convinced they were telling the truth. "Well, then, boys, that being the case, I reckon the smartest thing for me to do is get along up to San Antone. I don't figure it'll be any too healthy hanging around here."

I turned back to my pony. "If what you say is true,

then I got me a feeling Turk played us all for suckers."
I swung up into the saddle and looked down at them.
"But I'm not waiting around for a necktie party."

With a click of my tongue, I reined Hardhead onto
the San Antone road and headed northwest.

A few miles north of Limestone Hill, when I was
sure the boys weren't following me, I cut back east
for the *Diablo Paisaje*. I had a long ride ahead of me,
which was good because I had a heap of thinking to
do. Closecut and Oklahoma Fats had just stampeded
all my ideas across the prairie.

Chapter Seventeen

I never counted myself as too swift in the head, but the reading I did of Pa's books and magazines like *Harper's Monthly* and *Frank Leslie's Illustrated Monthly* always kept me thinking. So, on the long ride back to the Devil's Country that night, I dredged up everything that I could remember over the last three or four weeks.

Then I started remembering a few things I had forgotten: remarks, explanations, actions. I also remembered the last comment Turk made before he headed for the sheriff's office that night. *"I reckon your cock-eyed idea about me about me and the boys rustling them forty head ain't worth two hoots and a holler now, huh, Bookbinder?"* When I put that remark with facts I knew for sure, the answer to the puzzle came out only one way, despite the number of times I rearranged the circumstances.

To verify my theory, I'd send Jim and Ben to scout every trail leading out of Sand Springs. If they couldn't find Turk's trail out of the small town, then I had a hunch who was behind the whole thing. I didn't know why, but I reckoned the 'why' would come later. All I had to do now was wait until I could find out what the two young scouts would be able to tell me.

I rode through the night. The ranch was dark when I pulled up on a ridge overlooking the valley. I studied the sleeping ranch, remembering the signal I had failed to arrange. What if the sheriff were waiting? What if Matilda and Beth were in jail with Jim and Ben? What if one of them had been injured?

My brain reeled.

I couldn't take a chance on walking into an ambush, not with the shaky theory I had. No one would listen. I had to have solid proof.

Leaving Hardhead behind in a patch of oaks above the springhouse, I eased down to the river. I paused, noting the flat prairie and lack of hiding places. Even in the starlight, the prairie was a contrast of relief. Darker objects provided clear silhouettes against the bluish background provided by the stars.

I pulled some underbrush from the bank and waded into the shallow river, planning on using shrubs to break my outline. Maybe I could spot something as I drifted past.

The artesian water was like ice, taking my breath away when I first entered. My muscles tensed, my skin shrunk, my breath came in gasps.

Forcing the freezing water from my thoughts, I pushed off and began floating a hundred yards down-river. The icy water cut through my flesh like knives, chilling me to the bone. Then I began growing numb.

That changed fast when I floated by a stump on the bank that actually turned out to be a guard. I started sweating. Deciding not to take a chance on slipping up to the house to see if Matilda, Beth, and the boys were there, I kept floating, and I kept my head down, buried in the underbrush until I was another hundred yards below the ranch.

Were they under guard in the house, or had they escaped?

Easing from the icy water, I swung wide, reaching the small copse of oak in which I had tied Hardhead. I headed for the escarpment.

I rode north at a gallop. My pulse raced. This time, no one would be waiting to show me the trail to the escarpment. I remembered the strange track in the soft soil. I'd never before seen anything like it. And the smell . . . like death.

In the distance, a coyote howled. Closer, a symphony of crickets chirruped. Overhead, an owl swept past, the wind swishing past his wings. Abruptly, a jackrabbit burst from a bunch of switchgrass at my feet. Hardhead crowhopped, almost popping me from the saddle. I yanked on the reins and shouted. He steadied, and I tried to slow my own breathing back down out of the heart attack range.

Slowly, a dark line emerged from the horizon, a façade of shadows deep and black, growing ever larger and ominous as I drew closer. I had an idea where I would hit the *Paisaje* and the direction I would have to take for the escarpment. I just hoped I was right. I wasn't any too keen on wandering the narrow, twisting trails in the middle of the night with some unknown creature prowling the *Paisaje* for a tasty bite of grub.

While still a short distance from the *Paisaje*, I spotted the black silhouette of the escarpment to the northeast, just about where I figured. The trail into the escarpment was the same one we had taken out that morning. At least, I had that in my favor.

Finally, I reached the entrance to the trail. I reined up, shivering despite the sweat soaking my shirt. I waited for my eyes to adjust to the deeper shades of darkness. Leaning forward, I rubbed Hardhead's neck. "Okay, boy. It's up to you. Keep us on this trail."

He whinnied softly and arched his neck and dipped his head.

With a click of my tongue, I urged him into the obscurity of the gloomy shadows. The darkness caved in on me, enveloping me with a clammy closeness that seemed to be pressing in on me like the sides of a coffin.

Within moments of entering the primeval land, the

air grew still and silent, as if no creature dared make a sound. My thudding heart sounded like an Indian tom-tom to my ears, and each time I swallowed, the noise sounded like a rock dropped in a well of water.

Inside the tunnel-like trails, the only light came from the bluish shafts of starlight beaming through the overhead canopy of leaves and vines.

I gave my pony his head, knowing he would find his way along the dark trail. Slowly, we wound through the thick growth toward the escarpment, my ears straining to pick up the slightest sound other than my own breathing and the clatter of Hardhead's hoofs on the hardpan.

Then I stiffened.

The smell of death drifted to me on a random breeze, then was quickly dissipated by another faint breeze drifting up the trail. I listened hard, but all I could hear was my ragged breathing and Hardhead's hoofbeats.

Suddenly, a branch cracked off to my left.

Hardhead flinched, but kept moving along the trail. I shucked my six-gun and peered into the complete blackness off to my left. I kept listening for twigs snapping, limbs cracking, branches breaking, all tell-tale sounds of a charging animal. But the silence remained.

Then the smell came again, stronger this time.

Ahead, the escarpment rose from darkness.

Behind, a low rumble reverberated from the gloom. A branch snapped. I jerked around in my saddle, my heart thumping, my breath growing harsh. All I could see along the back trail was shafts of light penetrating the dark like blue stalks of sugar cane.

The escarpment loomed overhead now. I searched the gloom ahead frantically for the entrance to the cave. A yellow glow seemed to flicker through the darkness.

Another branch cracked, and then the crashing of a heavy body hurtling through the thick undergrowth exploded the silence.

At that moment, Hardhead jerked to the right as a hand grabbed the reins. A face appeared in the starlight. It was Ben. He whispered urgently. "Hold on, Charley. Hold on." He pulled us forward.

In the next instant, we charged through the entrance to the cave. Hardhead jerked back as we stumbled upon a small fire, but Ben hurried us around the blaze. Jim stood next to the tunnel wall, his arms loaded with dry brush. As we scraped past, he tossed the tangle of dried branches into the fire, which burst into leaping flames, sealing off the entrance.

From outside, a savage roar split the crackling of the fire. I twisted around and glimpsed the firelight flashing off the single blazing red eye of a shadowy creature stretching over twelve feet tall. In the next instant, it vanished.

I leaped from the saddle, dragging my Winchester with me and levering a cartridge into the chamber in the same motion. Jim held up his hand, halting me. "It is gone. The fire scared it off."

Ben tossed some more branches on the fire. "The Spirit of the *Mistai* has been outside tonight. Only the fire keeps it away."

While I never questioned a man's beliefs, I never could swallow the idea of ghosts. "That the one you mentioned before?"

Ben threw more logs on the fire, then turned back to me. He shrugged. "Yes. They are old stories, legends from our fathers. We call it a Spirit of the *Mistai*. Jim claims it is not a ghost. He believes it to be some kind of bear."

"But you?"

Ben looked at me somberly. "It is *Mistai*."

I had no idea what the creature was, but I knew it couldn't be a bear. "If it's a bear, where is its tracks? The sign I saw the first time I came here wasn't made by any kind of bear I've even seen. And this one . . . did you see him in the fire? I might be imagining things, but this . . . whatever it is, only had one eye." I remembered reading old stories about an ancient man with one eye, but until now, I'd always figured the story was just that, a story. Nothing more. "Did you see it?"

Ben shook his head. "No."

Jim looked up from stacking more logs next to the fire. "At least the creature has fled. What about Turk's men? Why did you not bring them back with you?"

I glanced into the darkness beyond the fire, crossing

my fingers that the creature would continue to be fearful of the blaze. "It's a long story. Let's go see Miss Matilda. I'll tell you what I found, and then we'll make us some plans and then come back and keep this fire going. We don't want any unwelcome guests tonight."

Chapter Eighteen

Miss Matilda and Beth awaited us in the great room. Over a mug of steaming sixshooter coffee, I related the events of my trip. "And I'm convinced they had no idea that Turk was planning on stealing the money. He sent them to Buffalo Wallow. Said he would follow them shortly, but he never showed up."

"So, he shot the sheriff and escaped with the money," said Matilda.

For a moment, I remained silent, studying the leaping flames in the fire.

Matilda spoke up. "Isn't that right, Charley? Turk shot the sheriff and escaped with the money?"

Ben stared at me curiously.

I shrugged. "When I backtracked, I found no sign of Turk cutting off from their trail. Then I found his bay on the outskirts of town grazing. To be sure, I

160

circled the town. There was no sign of a single pony leaving so he couldn't have stolen someone's horse." I paused, waiting for the inevitable question.

Matilda's forehead wrinkled in a frown. "Are you trying to say that Turk is still in town with the money?"

Pausing for another sip of coffee, I replied. "No. All I'm saying is that I found no sign of him leaving." I looked at the young men. "What I want you boys to do tomorrow is make sure I didn't miss anything. Throw a wide loop around the town. See if I missed any tracks, any sign of Turk."

Ben and Jim nodded.

Matilda studied me shrewdly. "You honestly don't believe Turk left town, do you?"

My only response was a grin. She made a second remark. "And you know where the money is, don't you?"

The others looked at me in surprise.

"No." I shook my head. "Not exactly. But if the boys prove I'm right about Turk's sign, then I think I can go straight to the money."

The boys rode out early next morning. I spent the day in the tunnel near the entrance, Winchester in hand, hoping they would return before dark. I had learned the night before that the middle of *Diablo Paisaje* was no place to be after the sun set.

Just before dusk, the boys rode in. Quickly, we built a fire, then headed upstairs.

"You were right, Charley," said Ben. "Two wagons left Sand Springs, but one went to the Carson Ranch, the other to the Circle Bar. Three drifters came in, but we found their sign as they moved out east. There was nothing more."

I leaned back against the wall of the cave and gave them a crooked smile. "Okay. Now listen carefully. Here's what we are going to do."

They scooted closer.

"Miss Matilda. Tomorrow around nine o'clock, I want you to go in and see George Markham."

"The mayor?" Matilda exclaimed.

"Yes. And I want you to have him call the sheriff, John Lewis at the general store, and the bartender. When they all get together, you tell them that I'm on the way into town with Turk and the twenty thousand dollars."

The four of them stared at me in surprise. Matilda pressed her fingers to her lips. "What about you? Where will you be?"

"With a witness," I said. "Someone the whole town will trust."

"Who?"

"Never mind. Just be there." I turned to Jim and Ben. "I want you boys to wait in the livery stable. Don't let anyone leave town after nine o'clock."

Miss Matilda asked. "What do you have in mind, Charley?"

I paused, on the one hand anxious to expound on my theory, on the other, fearful of their rejecting it.

"Well, it might be fuller of air than a tornado, but here's what I think happened."

When I finished, no one laughed.

Matilda frowned up at me. "You really believe that?"

I shrugged. "We'll find out tomorrow at nine o'clock."

Throughout the night, we heard the prowling of the great creature below, but the fire in the entrance kept it at bay. Sometime in the early morning hours, the beast moved away. Just as false dawn began graying the eastern sky, we rode out, single file, guns drawn in case the unknown beast was lying in wait for us.

We exited the *Dialblo Paisaje* without incident and headed south. A couple hours later, we rode up to Toby Reeves' place.

He was standing on the porch when we pulled up at the hitching rail. He wore his gunbelt, but made no attempt to go for his handgun when he saw me. He grinned ruefully. "I got to tell you, Charley. Either you got a lot of sand to come back here or else you ain't got nothing between those ears."

I rested my hands on the saddle horn and leaned forward. "I came to you, Toby, because I believe you're an honest man. Give me five minutes. If you think I'm still guilty, I'll go on into town with you without an argument. Can you deal with that?"

He studied me a moment. "What's the catch?"

"No catch." I shook my head.

Matilda spoke up. "Please, Mister Reeves. Listen to Charley." Beth nodded emphatically.

With a click of his tongue, he hooked his thumb over his shoulder. "Come on in. Coffee's hot."

I turned to Jim and Ben. "Ride on in, boys. We'll be in directly."

Steam rose from Toby Reeves' untouched cup of coffee as he stared at me in stunned disbelief. "That's impossible."

I leaned forward, resting my elbows on the sawbuck table. "Maybe it is, Toby, but even if you tossed me in a roomful of bobcats, I can't come up with another explanation. I might be completely wrong." I paused and glanced worriedly at Miss Matilda. She gave me a reassuring smile and laid her tiny hand on my arm. I continued. "And if I'm wrong, then what I'm doing is handing myself over to the hanging judge. I know that. Now, I laid out all my reasons for you. If you can juggle them around and come up with a different picture, I reckon I'd be much obliged."

He studied me for several long moments. "You really do believe what you're saying, don't you?"

"Yep." I held his eyes with mine and added, "I'm not a smart cowpoke, Toby, but I am honest. Go along with me on this. All you'll be out is a few more minutes."

Leaning back, he stared hard at me, then shifted his gaze to Miss Matilda. "How about you, Matilda? You believe him?"

Without hesitation, she nodded emphatically. "With all my heart, Toby. His guess might not be right, but I'd swear he wasn't mixed up with Turk in the robbery or the killing."

He rocked forward, the legs of his chair thumping against the puncheon floor. He stared at the steam rising from his coffee. Without a word, he rose, retrieved the whiskey from the cabinet, filled his and my cups, and said. "Okay. Let's see what happens."

I nodded to Matilda. "Nine o'clock. The mayor."

She grinned. "Don't worry. They'll be there."

Toby Reeves frowned. "You'll understand," I explained. "Now, let's go." We drained our cups.

We circled town and came in from the north, hiding in the livery until we spotted Matilda crossing the main street to the mayor's office. Scant minutes later, a slender man wearing checkered pants, a five-button vest, and a boiled shirt hurried up the street.

He ducked into the general store, then into the saloon, and finally crossed the street to the sheriff's office. Within seconds, the three men scurried over to the mayor's office.

I nudged Toby. "Let's go."

Staying in a crouch, we hurried across the field to the rear of the sheriff's office and quickly slipped inside. We paused, letting our eyes grow accustomed to the gloom of the room. The cells were empty as I guessed.

Toby shook his head. "I still can't believe it. Not Sheriff Turner."

Without answering, I hurried to the ladder leading up to the loft over the cells. "Quick. Before he gets back."

We clambered up the ladder and sprawled on our bellies in the dark, our eyes glued to the cracks between the planks of the loft's floor.

We lay without moving. I felt my heart thudding against my chest. Sweat soaked my shirt, stung my eyes. The temperature in the loft was over ninety despite it being so early in the morning.

We waited.

I tried to imagine the scene unfolding in the mayor's office. By now, Matilda had relayed the message. I guessed a short discussion would ensue as to their next step. I could imagine just how restless the discussion would make the sheriff, for somehow, he had to come up with an excuse that separated him from the others.

He had to see if the twenty thousand dollars was still where he hid it, and I was banking my life that the money, and Turk, were hidden here in the jail somewhere. And the only place was beneath the dilapidated puncheon floor.

But, if I was wrong. . . . I squeezed my eyes shut. I didn't want to think about that possibility.

The thudding of boot heels on the plank walk outside broke the steamy silence. The slab door creaked open. A fan of sunlight flashed across the wooden floor, then the door slammed.

For several moments, a tense silence filled the office. Sheriff Fred Turner's breath came in short, hard gasps. He remained motionless. In my mind's eyes, I saw him scanning the office, perhaps sensing something out of place. Had he spotted something out of kilter, something amiss? No. He couldn't. We had touched nothing, moved nothing.

The thin beads of sweat dripping from my face turned into rivulets, splashing on the loft floor. Beside me, Toby Reeves's breathing was shallow, rapid. I strained to peer through the cracks in the floor, cutting my eyes as sharply as I could in Turner's direction.

Suddenly, his feet moved within my sight. Mesmerized, I watched his boots cross the office and stop in front of the door of the end cell. He hesitated, then moved to the middle cell. The door creaked in protest when he opened it. He knelt directly under us, then hesitated once again. All I could see was his hat and his back.

He looked around, then quickly rose and strode across the office to the front door. I heard the locking peg drop into place. Moments later, I heard the thump of the peg drop in the back door, and then he returned to the cell.

He pulled out his Barlow knife and knelt. I glanced at Toby whose face was drawn tight with tension. I looked back as Sheriff Turner worked the blade of the knife between the planks in the floor.

And then I froze as the subdued sunlight caught a sparkle on a bead of sweat that had fallen between the cracks of the loft. It splattered on the floor behind Turner, but the Sheriff was too engrossed on prying loose the board to hear the faint noise.

I dared not move my body, but I lifted my head and eased it slightly to one side.

Without warning, another bead of sweat dropped, this time from Toby Reeves, splattering on the other side of the sheriff. I gulped. I wanted to catch the sheriff in the act, with the money, even with the body, for I figured Sheriff Fred Turner had not only killed George Wiggins, the cattle buyer, but Turk Warner, and placed the blame for the murder on the latter.

With a sharp pop, the plank snapped up.

Sheriff Turner paused, looked around, then quickly leaned forward and reached into the darkness beneath the floor. He straightened, in his hand a canvas bag. He opened it and pulled out a stack of greenbacks. He riffled the stack, then sat back on his heels.

Then a bead of sweat splattered on the floor in front of him. He stiffened momentarily, then relaxed. Slowly, he tied the neck of the bag and rose to his feet.

Without warning, he shucked his six-gun and whirled.

The Colt roared, spitting out 144-grain lead plums in belches of yellow fire. I rolled one direction, Toby the other, grabbing for his own handgun just as I was.

Leaping to my feet, I pumped three fast shots back through the floor. I heard Toby groan, but I was too busy dancing around, trying to dodge the lead dance partners Sheriff Fred Turner was throwing up at me. "Give it up, Sheriff," I shouted, trying to climb the back wall while throwing another slug in his direction.

Suddenly, I heard boot heels thudding across the floor. I jumped to the edge of the loft just as the sheriff threw open the front door. I snapped off a shot, tearing the bag of stolen money from his hand. He stopped, looked back at me.

Our eyes met. He reached for the bag, but I snapped off another shot, my last one.

He jerked his hand back and disappeared outside.

I started after him, then I heard Toby moan. I looked back. Blood had soaked his shirt near his belt. Holstering my Colt, I helped him down the ladder.

At that moment, the mayor and George Lewis, the owner of the general store, rushed in. "Bookbinder," exclaimed the mayor.

Toby shook his head. "The sheriff, Mayor. It was the sheriff. He shot me."

I began reloading my Colt.

George Lewis had stooped to retrieve the money from the floor. At that moment, Matilda, Beth, and the boys rushed in.

Toby continued, clenching his teeth. "We saw the sheriff get the money from where he hid it under the floor. Then he shot me."

Anxious to get after the sheriff, I helped Toby to a bunk. "Get the doc," I shouted.

The mayor frowned. "Toby is the doc."

"Oh. Yeah, yeah. Well, then get somebody else to help him." I headed for the door.

"Where are you going?" Matilda laid her hand on my arm and looked up at me in alarm.

"After the sheriff. He's getting away."

"Not by yourself."

"I go," said Ben.

Jim chimed in. "Me too."

I gave Miss Matilda a thin smile. "We'll be back."

Chapter Nineteen

Sheriff Turner headed north. No surprise. He planned on losing himself in the *Diablo Paisaje*.

Our ponies raced across the prairie like the summer wind, stretching out, pulling the miles in under their blazing hooves. Within minutes, we began spotting thin clouds of dust thrown up by Turner's gray. We were gaining.

A grim smile twisted my lips at the irony of the whole situation. To keep the town from hanging me, I had to ride into the den of an unknown creature twelve feet tall with one eye. Savage as a meat axe, it would tear me to pieces in an instant.

Some choice, a cauldron of boiling fat or the fire.

* * *

An hour passed, then another. Overhead, the sun reached its zenith. The clouds of dust drifted thicker, indicating we were closing in.

Back in the southwest, a line of gray clouds rolled over the horizon. Rumbles of thunder rolled across the prairie.

Finally, just as the ominous line of forest and boulder bordering the *Diablo Paisaje* rose from the short-grass prairie, we spotted a dark dot ahead of us.

"There he is," Ben shouted.

I dug my heels into Hardhead's flanks. With a grunt, he strained for another burst of speed. I shouted at the boys. "Jim, you stay on this side. If he comes back out, signal us."

By now, Turner had disappeared into the *Paisaje*. Jim pulled up while Ben and I raced inside. The trail forked abruptly. I slid Hardhead to a halt.

Ben stopped beside me.

A gust of wind rattled the leaves overhead. The boom of thunder reverberated through the *Paisaje*. Clouds rolled overhead.

"Which way, do you think?"

Leaning forward over the neck of his cow horse, he studied the trail at our feet. With a grin, he pointed to the left. "There. That trail. The sheriff, he went that way. The long way."

I frowned at him. He continued. "He makes a loop. This other trail—to the right, it goes straight."

I understood. "Okay," I said and nodded. "You take the short one. I'll follow him. If you spot him, signal."

With a wave of his hand, Ben turned down the narrow trail and quickly disappeared into the tangle of forest and boulders.

I dismounted and studied the sign in case the sheriff swung off the trail. The hard ground made reading sign difficult. I looked for some discerning mark, and found it with a missing nail in the shoe.

Patting Hardhead on the neck, I whispered. "Let's go now, boy. Nice and easy."

I followed the trail deeper into the *Paisaje*. The undergrowth grew thicker, the trees taller, and the rocky landscape rougher. Limbs hung over the trail, creating a gloomy tunnel that curved and twisted over the rugged ground.

An hour passed. Turner stayed ahead of me.

The clouds grew thicker. The thunder slowly rolled toward us.

Around every bend was a perfect spot for a bushwhacker to hide. I felt like I was playing Russian Roulette with five chambers loaded.

I rode with my Army Colt in my hand, hammer cocked. From time to time, I paused to listen, but other than the silence of the *Paisaje*, I heard nothing. I clung to Turner's trail with a pigheaded stubbornness that would have made any mule proud.

Ahead, a branch snapped.

I pulled up, eyes narrowed, peering into the luxuriant undergrowth before me. I strained to hear another sound. There was nothing but the silence of the wind rattling the leaves. Then I realized I had been holding my breath. I released it noisily and rolled my shoulders in an effort to relax my tense muscles.

Gently squeezing Hardhead's ribs with my knees, I continued on the trail. The trail started swinging back toward the escarpment. "So, that's what you're up to," I mumbled.

I stayed on his trail, pushing Hardhead faster. Behind me, thunder echoed across the prairie. I pulled up, staring into the cloud-darkened trail that stretched before me until it disappeared in the shadows.

I suppose it was the thunder that startled Hardhead. All I remember was an explosion and then the saddle came out from under me. I slammed to the ground. My head bounced off the hardpan. I fought against the blackness threatening to engulf me. Somewhere in far distance, I heard the thudding of hoofbeats, fading, fading, fading.

Then an excruciating pounding started in my head. From somewhere in the darkness surrounding me, I heard a voice. I flexed my fingers, realizing I still clutched my Colt. Willing my numbed body to move, I rolled off the trail, hoping to roll out of sight into the underbrush, worming as deep as I could.

I lay on my belly, fighting the waves of dizziness spinning in my head. I opened my eyes and blinked.

Through the thick tangle of branches and leaves, I spotted Sheriff Turner creeping along the side of the trail, gun in hand. I held my breath. His eyes moved like a weasel's, scanning the trail, searching for me.

Once our eyes seemed to meet. I tightened my finger on the trigger, but the sheriff moved on past, his feet crunching on the dried leaves and brittle branches.

When his back was to me, I spoke out. "Hold it right there, Sheriff. Don't turn around. I got the muzzle of this .44 lined up right on the middle of your back."

He froze, arms outstretched. He half turned his head.

I crawled from the underbrush and tried to stand. My head spun. The blow to back of my skull had made me weak as pond water. I grabbed the trunk of a small sweetgum, steadying myself. "Now, drop the gun and turn around."

Turner turned to face me. His eyes narrowed. He still held the Colt in his hand.

"I said drop it, Sheriff. Now." I should have seen his muscles tense, but everything was swimming before my eyes.

He nodded slowly. "Sure, Charley. Whatever you say." The handgun clattered to the ground. I looked down at it, and that was all he needed. He leaped forward, lowering his head like a charging bull.

I squeezed off a shot, but his head slammed into my belly, knocking me backward. My handgun went spinning into the underbrush. I stumbled, catching my heel on a stump and sprawling flat on my back.

Sheriff Turner stomped at my head. I swung my arm, catching his swinging boot and spinning him around. I pulled my knees to my chest and lashed out with both feet at his leg still planted on the ground.

I caught his knee, and with a loud curse, he fell backward. He spun on his back and kicked at me with his feet. I did the natural thing. I kicked back at him. He kicked back, and I returned the favor, and for the next few moments, we were just grown-up children kicking at each other.

As if by signal, we both jumped to our feet.

Lips twisted in a snarl, Turner threw a roundhouse right. I ducked, stepped forward, and ripped a left hook into his kidney. He grunted and staggered back, then lunged forward, throwing another looping right that caught me on my right temple. Flashing stars exploded in my eyes. My sight blurred. I swung a left in desperation, grunting with satisfaction when my knuckles smashed against his skull.

Another blow caught me just above my right eye. I swung blindly, and took another sharp blow to my head.

Shaking my head, I stepped back and focused on the sheriff.

He had dropped into a crouch, his fists knots of bone and flesh. I saw smears of my blood on his knuckles. The snarl on his lips reminded me of a rabid dog. He growled. "You no-good, dirty—"

I busted him between the eyes with a straight right, wincing when my knuckles seemed to bend under the blow. I pivoted on my right foot and threw another left hook, this one at his unprotected jaw.

With a grunt, he deflected the hook with his right forearm and threw a left, straight from the shoulder. I tried to sidestep, but his bony knuckles caught the point of my cheekbone, stinging like the blazes. Blood spurted from the split skin.

I slammed his arm aside and thudded a solid left to his heart.

He grimaced and staggered back.

I charged, pumping lefts and rights into his belly which had gone to fat after years of poker, loafing, and five meals a day.

His fingers clawed at my eyes, trying to jab them from their sockets. One poked into my mouth, and I bit it.

He screamed and jerked it back, loosening a couple of my teeth in the process. His face turned livid with rage. He threw out his arms and leaped at me, pinning my arms to my side. He lifted me off the ground and squeezed.

I tried to twist my arms free, but his thick arms held me tight. Abruptly, I popped my head forward, slamming my forehead against his nose.

The sheriff screamed and grabbed his nose. Blood squirted between his fingers. With a grimace of triumph, I leaped at him. With a curse, he kicked at me, catching me in the groin. I doubled over, grimacing at the pain, at the same time expecting a boot heel to my skull.

Muttering curses, Sheriff Turner staggered backward, then turned and shuffled awkwardly down the trail. I rolled into a sitting position, my teeth clenched against the excruciating pain. Nausea churned my stomach.

By now, shadows filled the trail, and the last of the sunlight glowed dimly behind the gray clouds. Gagging, I staggered to my feet. I was hesitant to follow the sheriff. I had no weapon, and I wasn't anxious to stumble onto him again without a handgun.

A rumble of thunder reverberated through the forest.

Hastily, I searched the underbrush along the side of the trail. Luck smiled, for within seconds, I found my Army Colt. Then I hurried after Sheriff Turner.

Ahead, the escarpment loomed.

If he made it inside, we'd never find him. There were too many tunnels, offshoots, too many places for an ambush.

Abruptly, a guttural roar followed by a terrified scream and three fast shots broke the silence of the oncoming night. I broke into a run as a cacophony of frightened screams and angry growls and gunshots echoed through the dusk.

I rounded a bend and skidded to a halt. My eyes bulged.

A grotesque creature reared upright, stretching over twelve feet in height. White fangs glistened in contrast to a dark, shiny face from which peered a single eye. A grizzly bear, its head and muzzle seared to leather from fire, roared. The entire *paisaje* seemed to tremble.

For a moment, I stood transfixed, unable to believe my eyes. Then Sheriff Turner fired again at the gigantic creature lumbering toward him. The click of Sheriff Turner's gun on an empty cartridge snapped me from the shock that had mesmerized me.

Frantically, the sheriff grabbed fresh slugs from his gunbelt.

I shouted. "Run! You hear me? Run!"

The creature waved its huge front legs, and I saw the legs had no toes. The fire that had seared the legs up to the knees had also burned the creature's pads, scarring them to leather. Without warning, the beast dropped to all fours and charged the sheriff.

I backed up. "Run!" I shouted again and started pumping .44 slugs into the charging beast.

I heard Sheriff Tucker curse softly as he snapped the cylinder shut and raised his handgun.

When he looked up, it was into the red eye of a savage grizzly. Drool dripped from the fangs in its gaping mouth.

The sheriff threw up an arm to deflect the bear's lunge, but the roaring grizzly caught the sheriff's throat. He screamed and emptied his handgun into the ferocious brute that shook him like a dirty strip of wet rag.

I fired my last three shots into the growling creature.

From behind me, another gun fired, a rifle. A second rifle joined in from the other side of the snarling beast.

With a final snap of its head, the creature whipped the limp body of Sheriff Turner into the underbrush beside the trail. It reared on its hind legs, waving its stumps defiantly in the air.

I clicked on an empty cylinder. Quickly, I backed away, reloading as fast as I could.

The creature dropped to all fours, stood unsteadily a moment, snapped its grotesque head from side to side two or three times, then collapsed.

As I finished reloading, Ben and Jim appeared, Winchesters in hand. I grinned weakly. "Mighty glad you boys was around. Things were getting sticky around here."

And then the clouds opened, washing off the countryside with a cleansing rain.

Chapter Twenty

The rain had subsided and clouds had blown away and the Big Dipper indicated midnight by the time we reached Sand Springs with the sheriff's body. We skirted town and pulled up at Toby Reeves' spread.

Minutes later, John Lewis and Mayor George Markham had gathered in the Reeves' kitchen with Toby and his family, Matilda, Beth, the boys, and me. Mrs. Reeves had boiled a pot of sixshooter coffee. A swallow of that thick concoction of syrup was enough to keep a jasper's eyes open for a week. And if that didn't do the trick, then one or two generous dollops of whiskey dumped in the coffee helped.

John Lewis arched an eyebrow. "A grizzly, you say? We'd often wondered just what was out there."

"That's what made the odd tracks. Looked like he was caught in a fire and it burned his paws and face."

"That must have been during the wildfire eight or nine years back," said Toby Reeves. "The entire *Paisaje* burned off."

Miss Matilda dabbed at her eyes. "The poor creature must have suffered terribly."

I nodded, saying nothing. It was hard to feel sorry for a beast that only an hour or so earlier was dead set on ripping me to pieces.

"But what I don't understand, Charley," said Mayor Markham, "is how you figured out what the sheriff was up to."

I leaned forward and spiked my coffee with whiskey. "I didn't at first. Then the day we brought the cattle in, Turk made the remark that I was all cockeyed about Ben and Jim accusing him and his boys of rustling forty head of cattle. You see, Turner was the only one I had talked to about that."

Toby nodded. "So the only way Turk could have known that was if Sheriff Turner had told him."

"Yeah." I sipped the coffee. "And the sheriff had told me earlier that he hadn't said a word to Turk for months."

The store owner, John Lewis, frowned. "That didn't seem like much to go on, Charley."

"There's more. You remember when we got to the sheriff's office that night, Toby? The sheriff said that Turk and his boys stole the money and shot Wiggins. Best I remember, he said *That's when they shot Wiggins. Closecut and Oklahoma Fats was right behind. They closed the door and started shooting. Turk* grabbed the money, and they hightailed it out the back door."

Toby Reeves leaned forward. "Yeah. I remember."

"According to Fats and Closecut, they were never in the sheriff's office. Turk came out back and told them to meet at Buffalo Wallow."

"Naturally, we all believed the sheriff. But then these two boys and me only found sign of two men leaving town that night, not three. Jim and Ben followed the trail on to Buffalo Wallow, but I backtracked. I found Turk's bay grazing just outside of town. In fact, that's when the townspeople spotted me and you old boys gave chase."

A glimmer of understanding began surfacing in their eyes. I continued. "You remember the gunshot wound to the sheriff's leg?"

Mayor Markham shrugged. "Yeah. It scorched his denims. Almost set them on fire. So what?"

Toby answered for me. "Mayor, the only way you scorch a piece of clothing with a gunshot is if you hold the muzzle against the cloth itself, or close to it."

I continued. "Which is just what Sheriff Turner did. He had Turk tell Closecut and Oklahoma Fats to meet him in Buffalo Wallow. I'm guessing that Turk planned on him and the sheriff splitting the twenty thousand. But the sheriff doublecrossed Turk and shot himself to make it look like Turk had tried to kill him."

Mayor Markham eyed me narrowly. "What did he do with Turk's body?"

I sipped the coffee again. "What did he do with the money?"

"Huh?"

Toby grinned. "Under the floor. He buried Turk under the floor."

"That's what I would guess," I replied, draining my coffee. "You can yank some of them boards up by hand. I figure he hid him, and then later, after everybody was gone, dug a hole under the floor and buried the body."

John Lewis pushed back from the table. "Then let's find out."

Turk Warner's body was wrapped in canvas and buried three feet deep. We all stood around, staring down at the body. "Well, you were right, Charley," whispered the mayor.

I looked at him. "What about Miss Matilda's cattle?"

The mayor shrugged. "Don't worry. The company Wiggins worked for will still buy them. The mortgage will be paid off, and the Great Northeast Land and Mortgage Company will have to cry in their beer."

"Well then, that's what I was supposed to do. I guess that takes care of my time in jail, huh?"

My ex-poker playing friends laughed. John Lewis grinned at me. "Reckon so, Charley. I guess you'll be moving on now, huh?"

"Yep," said Toby. "And don't forget, you got over nine hundred dollars coming."

Before I could answer, Miss Matilda spoke up. "Hold on, John Lewis and Toby Reeves. When Sheriff Turner brought Charley Bookbinder out to my place to go to work, the agreement was for thirty-four days. Isn't that right, Charley?"

She looked me squarely in the eyes, a funny little smile on her lips. I nodded. "Yes, Ma'am. I reckon so, but—"

She interrupted. "No buts. We agreed on thirty-four days, and thirty-four days it is. We still have six to go."

I frowned at her. What the Sam Hill was going on? And then her smile broadened. I glanced at Beth beside, and then the boys standing behind Miss Matilda. I might not be real swift between the ears sometime, but I figured out just what she was saying.

"Well?" She feigned a stern expression on her face. "I still have work to do, and I need a strong back now that my other hands are gone."

Toby Reeves grinned at me. I nodded. "Yes, Ma'am, I reckon an agreement is an agreement. I wouldn't be wanting to break it. Six days it is, Miss Matilda."

She tilted her chin and her smile broadened. "Then let's go." She turned on her heel and headed for the door.

I hesitated until John Lewis put his boot in my rear. "I'm coming, Miss Matilda," I said.

Over her shoulder, she said. "You might as well start calling me Mattie, Charley."

I winked at Mayor Markham. "Okay, Mattie. I been thinking about all the work at your spread. I might need a little more time than just six days."

She paused at the door and looked back. "I reckon we can work that out, Charley. I reckon we can work that out."